Premature Holiness

Five Weeks at the Ashram

A Novel

by Gudjon Bergmann

www.flamingleafpress.com

Premature Holiness: Five Weeks at the Ashram

This is a work of fiction. Names, characters, places, and incidents are either a product of the author's imagination or are used ficticously. Any resemblance to actucal persons, living or dead, events, or locales is entirely coincidental.

Published by Flaming Leaf Press, 2016
www.flamingleafpress.com

www.authorbergmann.com

ISBN: 978-0-9973012-2-9

To my gurus, who have been
perfectly imperfect

GB

Prologue

His head was spinning. How? How could he have let this happen? The bedroom looked like it always did. Colorful pictures of Vishnu and Lakshmi hung on the walls. The queen-sized bed stood in the middle of the floor, shrouded with a net canopy. His meditation pillows were stacked in a corner next to his dresser. Burned down candles and withering fresh flowers adorned his altar, his refuge. Yet, the familiarity did not calm him.

How could he? He was the guru, the role model.

It was one mistake. One.

He had tried to live a good life, had taught others to live ethically, had served with a pure heart, had helped thousands of people transform their lives, but now, one mistake, one stain, threatened his reputation, his livelihood, his very existence. An hour earlier, he'd been involved in a graduation ceremony. A knock on the door had interrupted the proceedings. It was a sound he would never forget.

He sat down on their bed, his back straight, his feet barely touching the floor, his arms hanging by his sides, and stared at the wall, immobile. The midday sun, shining through the wooden Venetian blinds, gently lit the room.

Then, without warning and to his own amazement, his body began to shake. He was crying. Crying. For the first time since he was ten years old. He had long prided himself of rising above emotions, of living in complete equilibrium, of steering clear of highs and lows, but now his feelings overwhelmed him.

Noises coming from outside caught his attention. There was shouting, screaming, and car doors slamming, engines revving up and tires spinning in the gravel as vehicles sped down the driveway. He gathered himself, stood up, and walked to the window. Of course. They were all leaving. Who could blame them?

When the dust settled, only one person stood, aghast, in the parking lot. His right-hand man had decided to stay. Was it due to loyalty or did the young man not know where to go?

Staggering back to bed, he collapsed on the floor. Death, take me now, he thought, but he wasn't dying. No. Emotions had simply overwhelmed him, and he had lost the capacity to stand for a moment. He rolled onto his back on the creaky wooden floor and covered his eyes with his hands. No. He wasn't dying. Death would've been an easy out. If there really was such a thing as karma, he needed to face the consequences of his actions.

The chain of events flashed over and over in his mind. The knock on the door. The news. The horrible, gut-wrenching news. He couldn't have seen this coming, could he?

It didn't matter. He was at fault. He had triggered the domino effect. The stain on his character was no longer a tiny speck on an otherwise white background. No, it was growing and had turned into a black hole that was devouring everything in its path.

Chapter One

Five weeks earlier

"This is it, sir," the shuttle driver said as he stopped the car.

"Where is the house?"

"It must be somewhere behind those trees, sir. This looks to be a fairly large plot of land."

"Aren't you going to drive me up to the house?"

"No, sir. In the shuttle business, we go from curb to curb. This is the closest I can take you."

"What if this isn't the right address? It took us a while to find this place. You said yourself that you aren't a hundred percent sure."

"This is the address, sir. The number is on the mailbox. I just didn't see it when we passed this way before," the driver said as he unloaded two bags and a backpack onto the street. "Thank you for your business, but I must keep moving. I have several other passengers to drop off in the area."

The shuttle sped away.

At six-feet-two, lean, with short-cropped hair and graying stubble, Bjarni Jóhann Helgason stood at the end of a white gravel driveway, sweating profusely in the Florida midday sun, wearing a t-shirt, jeans, and trainers. Temperatures were in the high nineties, and the humidity was near eighty percent. He strapped on his backpack, grabbed his suitcases, and started walking up the gravel path, flanked by unruly vegetation.

The chirps, buzzing, and hissing sounds coming from the flora caused his imagination to run wild. He envisioned a den of snakes, poisonous spiders, and wasp hives surrounding him.

Would they attack?

He was a long way from home and tired after hours upon hours of traveling. For precaution, he stayed in the middle of the road as he took one sweaty step after another towards his supposed destination.

Approximately thirty yards from where he'd been dropped off, the gravel road swerved to the left. On both sides of that bend, which marked the entrance to the estate, was a high barrier of trees. Having passed the entryway, he saw two roofs, forty yards or so ahead.

This must be it, he thought as he quickened his step.

Although a marathon runner, he was not used to this kind of heat and humidity. His underwear was soaking wet, and his dry fit t-shirt was drenched, although it didn't show thanks to the unique material.

He held his smaller bag in his left hand while he dragged the bigger one with his right up the gravel road, rolling it over bump after gravelly bump, regularly needing to stop and level it off with both hands when the bag almost tipped over. He had packed enough stuff to last him five weeks. That was how long he was going to be staying at this place—if, in fact, this was the place.

As he drew closer, he noticed a large parking lot and discovered three houses, not two as he had previously thought.

There was a one-story white building with a double door entrance in the middle that appeared to be the main hall. In front of it were beautifully arranged flowerbeds and a red brick walkway connecting it to buildings on either side.

To the left was a yellow two-story house that must have been a barn at some point. Huge barn doors were facing the parking lot and a small entrance in the back was connected to the red brick walkway.

To the right was a bright orange cottage, no more than one thousand square feet.

The walkway between the three houses was covered with a wire framework that had weaving vegetation growing on top of it, providing a makeshift roof.

Making a best guess estimate, he headed for the main building. He set his bags up against the wall, took off his shoes—there was a shoe rack out front indicating that one should do that—and peered inside. He was greeted by a hallway that ran straight through the house to a screen door that opened into the backyard. To his left was a dining hall and to his right a large carpeted room with no furniture in it.

"Hello? Is anybody here?"

No answer.

With caution, he walked into the dining room. In one corner there was a fully equipped kitchen with hotel style appliances. The floor was covered with black and white marble colored linoleum on which stood nine one-foot high dining room tables lined up in three rows. There were no chairs anywhere, only several thin pillows stacked up against the wall. Indian music was playing on a tiny radio on the windowsill.

"Hello!" he called again.

No answer.

He left the dining room and crossed the hall into the carpeted room. On the walls hung several pictures of a blue character with distinct Indian characteristics. In some of them, he was playing the flute, in others, he was surrounded by a group of women, and, in still others, he was depicted as a blue baby suckling on the teat of a cow. In the far end of the room was a small wooden stage, above which hung a picture of an older Indian gentleman with long white beard and hair, dressed in orange robes. Two sizable empty vases flanked the stage.

By now, he was fairly sure that he was in the right place. It was just a matter of finding someone to confirm it. He hurried out, into the natural steam bath that awaited him, put on his trainers and walked towards the two-story barn-like structure to the left of the main house. Again, a shoe rack indicated that he should take off his shoes, so he did.

He entered a seating area with two glass coffee tables that had pillows stacked around them on the wooden floor. There was a staircase to the second floor on his left and directly ahead there was a hallway with several doors opening to both sides.

"Hello?!"

The frustration in his voice was building. He was tired and sweaty. The welcoming committee was nowhere to be seen.

He walked down the hall that led to the sleeping quarters and counted six bedrooms. He was in dire need of a restroom, but could not find one.

Heading back outside, he put on his trainers one more time. In Iceland, he would have urinated in the bushes without any qualms, but the insect noises that were coming from all around him were a definite deterrent, plus, he'd been told that indecent exposure laws in the USA were relatively strict and that knowledge gave him pause as well.

Looking to his left, he noticed a walkway in between the main house and the sleeping quarters that led into a large field behind the houses. The field was filled fruit trees of some sort. He still had one house left to explore, so, instead of venturing into the field, he walked back past the main house towards the orange cottage and knocked on the door.

No answer.

Another knock.

This time a slight Indian man, no taller than five feet, with scruffy, long, black, silver-streaked hair and long beard, wearing white hemp clothes and no shoes, came to the door.

"Yogi Krishna Soham," the Icelandic man cried, recognizing the Indian gentleman from the pictures on his website. "I am so glad that it's you. I was afraid that I was in the wrong place. My name is Bjarni or BJ. I came all the way from Iceland to attend your five hundred hour yoga teacher training. I emailed someone called Govinda who told me that it was okay that I arrive one day early, so, here I am."

Yogi Krishna Soham did not answer. Rather he looked like he had been rudely interrupted. Without a word, he pointed BJ towards the other houses.

"I've looked, but there is no one there," BJ responded, confused by the behavior.

Still, Yogi Krishna Soham did not talk. Instead, he pointed

towards the other houses and shook his hand, like he was ushering BJ away. Then, without warning, he closed the door.

Not understanding what had just happened, BJ made his way back to the other two houses, utterly bewildered. He shouted periodically but got no response. His bladder felt like it was about to burst. He had to relieve himself, bugs or no bugs, laws or no laws.

He ran towards the walkway that led into the field behind the houses. There he discovered an additional structure — a row of stalls, roofed with corrugated sheet metal. Bathrooms! After using one of them, BJ walked back into the field, feeling lighter. He couldn't help but smile. Right then, he heard another toilet flush. Out of one of the stalls walked a young Caucasian man, probably in his late twenties. He was wearing white clothes, similar to what Yogi Krishna Soham had been wearing, and was about six-feet tall, extremely thin for his height.

"Govinda?" BJ guessed as he extended his hand.

"Yes," the man answered.

"My name is Bjarni Jóhann Helgason. You can call me BJ. I am here for the yoga teacher training — all the way from Iceland."

"Yes, yes, welcome," Govinda replied in a thick Germanic accent. "I remember our email correspondence. Welcome to the ashram."

"I can't say that I feel very welcome," BJ blurted out in frustration. "I went to the orange cottage, and Yogi Krishna Soham didn't speak a word to me, just ushered me away and slammed the door."

"That's my fault," Govinda replied hastily, looking like he would get into trouble for it later. "I should have been at the house to greet you. You see, today is Gurudev's day of silence. He and his wife always observe a day of silence before the start of a new yoga teacher training. He meant no disrespect."

"Oh, I didn't know that."

"How could you?" Govinda replied and laughed nervously. "It's quite alright. Let me help you get settled in. How was your trip?"

"Long and tiring. I flew overnight and spent several hours at the

Orlando airport before I could fly to Miami. Then the shuttle driver dropped me off at the curb. I am drenched in sweat. A nap and a shower would serve as a welcome relief," BJ replied.

"We will make that happen Bjarni—that is how you say it, correct?"

"Pretty close. You must be from Europe. I haven't met a single American who can pronounce my name yet, which is why I tell everyone to call me BJ."

"Yes, I am from Switzerland," Govinda replied.

"I thought you'd be an Indian, like Yogi Krishna Soham, because of your name, Govinda."

"Govinda is my spiritual name. My birth name was Herman Keller, but when I became Gurudev's disciple and moved here, he gave me a new spiritual name."

"You live here full-time?"

"Yes and no. Unfortunately, I have to travel back to Switzerland every six months to renew my visa, but I stay here for as long as I can and as often as I can."

The two men walked to the front of the main building, grabbed BJ's bags and headed for the sleeping quarters.

"Is it always this hot and humid here?" BJ asked.

"Only during summer," Govinda replied. "It's unusually hot for June. It should cool down a little when we get the afternoon showers. You can count on them like clockwork. They usually arrive between two and four."

BJ looked at his watch. The local time was one-thirty.

"You don't sound like you are from Iceland," Govinda remarked. "I have a thick accent when I speak English, but I can hardly detect yours."

"I traveled a lot when I was a kid, plus, I mostly watch movies and TV shows in English. Spending a summer at an English school run by Americans in Austria when I was fifteen probably made the biggest difference, almost erased my accent, but most people in Iceland speak fairly good English."

8

"I see," Govinda replied.

They entered the sleeping quarters.

"Since you are the first one to arrive, you get the privilege of choosing a room for the men. There are only four men enrolled in the yoga teacher training so the four of you will be bunking together."

"What about you?" BJ asked. "Where do you sleep?"

"I have a small room upstairs," Govinda replied.

"Well, you know this place. What room would you suggest I take?"

"This place is going to be full of women within twenty-four hours, so I would take the most private room, away from this area here, where they gather and talk, talk, talk, all the time. The most private room would be this one here," Govinda said, as he walked down the hall and entered the last room on the left, "right underneath my room, so you won't be disturbed by any ruckus from above. Plus, there is only one room next to it."

Walking back down the hall, Govinda asked: "If you don't mind me asking, why did you pick this yoga teacher training? You seem different from the people who usually come here."

"My girlfriend in Iceland is a yoga teacher and early next year we plan to open a yoga studio together. I used to work as an accountant, but now I am a full-time investor. The yoga studio is my next investment. Even though she is my girlfriend, I follow the Buffett rule and usually don't invest in anything that I don't understand. That is why I decided to attend a yoga teacher training."

BJ was startled by the sound of thunder.

"Why I chose this one," he continued after steadying himself, "because I wanted something authentic and this program with Yogi Krishna Soham seemed both genuine and immersive. I like the idea of getting the five hundred hour accreditation in five weeks."

The rain started coming down hard.

"To tell you the truth, I wasn't entirely convinced until after I read his book, *How to Build a Better Pose*, which is the most sensible treatise on yoga postures I have read so far."

Again, BJ was shocked by a loud crackle of thunder. It shook the building.

"You weren't kidding about the thunderstorms, were you?" he asked, trying to laugh it off.

"No. They arrive here like clockwork."

"We don't get any thunderstorms in Iceland, so I can't say I am used to this."

"After a few days, you will be. Just try to stay inside when there is lightning."

Govinda prepared to leave, then added: "You can join us for dinner at six. The showers are outside, behind the toilets. Be on the lookout for spiders and snakes. Most of them are not poisonous."

"Spiders? Snakes? Really? How am I supposed to know which ones are poisonous and which ones aren't?" BJ asked incredulously.

"There is a little booklet underneath the coffee table that explains the difference—but don't worry about it. I've been here off and on for two years and never seen a poisonous snake or spider. The worst that has happened to me is the occasional insect bite, either from a fire ant or wasp."

"Fire ant?"

"Yes, they are small red ants that you will find out in the field. Their bites sting quite a bit, so if they crawl on you I suggest that you find a hose and spray them off with water immediately, but as I said, don't worry about it too much. Enjoy your stay here. This is a blessed place."

Govinda left, and BJ got settled in his room. He chose a bottom bunk and unpacked some of his clothes, arranging them in two of the eight shelves in the room. He left the other six empty for his roommates who would arrive tomorrow, along with the rest of the students.

Dinner was served at six o'clock that Friday night by Lilavati, Yogi Krishna Soham's wife. She was smaller than her husband—at just under five-feet—and wore a traditional Indian sari, blue with yellow markings. By all standards, she was severely overweight. To

BJ that was inexplicable. How could the yoga master's wife be fat? It was one of many questions that plagued him, the foremost one being, had he made a giant mistake by coming here?

In silence, the four of them sat on the floor by one of the low dining room tables and ate soupy vegetables in a delicious curry sauce, with rice and homemade flat bread. Yogi Krishna Soham, Lilavati, and Govinda ate with their hands. BJ tried to emulate, but when it was clear that he wasn't getting the hang of it, Govinda gave him a fork and spoon. No one made eye contact during dinner. The only sounds were slurping and chewing noises. It was the strangest dinner setting BJ had ever experienced.

After dinner, BJ went straight to his room. The ceiling fan was rotating at full speed, yet the muggy air was palpable. He kept sweating, even after taking a shower. Lying in bed, he got out his copy of *How to Build a Better Pose* by Yogi Krishna Soham—the book that had seduced him to come here—and read the introduction:

This is Hatha Yoga. Ha means sun. Tha means moon. Hatha Yoga is Yin and Yang. Its goal is to create balance. Too much strength and the body is stiff. Too much flexibility and the body is continually restless. With the proper practice of Hatha Yoga, one should be able to assume a near perfect meditation posture, firm but relaxed, steady but not stiff. There should be flow in the stillness. The practice of Hatha Yoga has overall health benefits that can alleviate many of the lifestyle diseases people suffer from in our society, including digestive disorders, back pain, stress, anxiety, and sleep problems.

The text was to the point and practical, unlike what he had experienced thus far during his first day at the ashram. He couldn't help but imagine what the rest of the five weeks would be like. That triggered mixed emotions. He wanted this to be a good experience, but...

After tossing and turning for two hours, BJ finally fell asleep.

Chapter Two

The rest of the students arrived on Saturday morning, and the program officially started at one o'clock on Saturday afternoon with a short orientation from Govinda. He explained that the goal was to complete one hundred hours of training per week. Therefore, the schedule started at six o'clock every morning and went until nine-thirty in the evening, with lights out at ten-thirty. The ashram provided two vegetarian meals per day, breakfast and dinner. Everyone was required to perform one hour of service, or seva, daily and got two hours of free time between twelve and two in the afternoon. Students were not allowed to bring alcohol, tobacco, guns, meat, drugs or electronics onto the premises, and sex was not allowed, even for couples. Failure to comply would result in expulsion without a refund. Govinda put these rules forth like a drill instructor.

Because of the electronics ban, BJ asked if he could use the ashram phone to call his girlfriend and children in Iceland, using an international phone card, but got a cold no for an answer, was told that maybe there was a payphone near the local strip mall.

During the next break, BJ leaned over to his roommate, Kurt.

"I am forty-six. I think I am too old for this," he said.

"Too old to follow rules?"

"No, too old to be treated like a kid by a kid."

"I don't mind the rules," Kurt replied, "I just wish I'd known there were no special provisions for vegans like myself."

BJ inquired briefly about the difference between vegetarianism and veganism—declaring that he was a proud carnivore—but their conversation was cut short when Yogi Krishna Soham entered the room and sat on the stage in full lotus pose, dressed in all white. On either side of him were two big vases filled with freshly cut flowers. Candles had been lit during the break. The setting was picturesque and had the desired effects. The group seemed mesmerized.

Silver streaks in his black beard and hair, along with a receding hairline, were indicators of Yogi Krishna Soham's age, but the skin on his brown face was smooth as a baby's bottom and the whites in his hazel brown eyes were almost fluorescent, making him look younger than he actually was. His spine was completely straight, his chest open, and his arms relaxed. He smiled and looked attentively around the room, stopping momentarily to greet each of the sixteen students with what could only be described as a tender loving gaze. It was evident that he belonged on that stage, unlike his young right-hand man who was now nowhere to be seen.

The students sat still, looking at the Indian yoga master, waiting for him to speak, but he maintained silence and kept looking attentively at the group with a gentle smile. Little by little, every person in the room began smiling as well. After five minutes or so, some of the students started giggling while others began to snigger nervously, clearly unaccustomed to receiving such attention in absolute silence. Finally, the hush was broken.

"Hello," a tan, muscular woman in trendy orange and gray activewear blurted out nervously. "My name is Poppy Williams."

"Hello, miss Poppy," the master responded in a melodic voice with a slight Indian accent. "Welcome to my yoga teacher training," he added, looking directly at her.

"Thank you," she replied, blushing slightly.

"Welcome, to all of you," he said, looking up. "Forgive my long silence. I was immersed in greeting the Atman within each and every one of you."

He placed his hands in prayer pose.

"Namaste!" he said.

"Namaste!" the group responded, also placing their hands in prayer pose.

"That means I greet the Atman, the divine light, the soul, the self, the spirit within you. When you say Namaste, you are not talking about someone's personality or mind or body, no, you are addressing the essence that resides in all of us. The divine center around which all else revolves."

Again, he looked around the room with his hands in prayer pose.

"With understanding, say, Namaste!"

"Namaste!" the group responded and bowed.

"Turn to your neighbor, look into their eyes and say Namaste! Greet everyone. Honor the light within each and every person in this room."

The room burst into sound.

"Namaste! Namaste! Namaste!" everyone said.

Some performed the greeting solemnly, others sheepishly, yet others skeptically, but everyone did it. Finally, the group settled down and returned their attention to the stage.

"As you know, my name is Yogi Krishna Soham, but that hasn't always been the case. I was born sixty-five years ago in Porbandar, a coastal city in Gujarat in India, the birthplace of the great Mahatma Gandhi. My birth name was Gopal Dhaduk. My family was very religious and sent me to study with my guru, Swamidev, when I was only seven years old. Back then, I awoke at five in the morning and bathed in cold water from the well, then ran to my guru's house and practiced yoga postures with him until seven, which was when I went off to school. He never taught us directly, rather by example. We simply followed along with whatever he was doing. Then, in the evenings, I spent time at his feet, learning about the spiritual and philosophical aspects of yoga."

Yogi Krishna Soham pointed to the picture above his head and continued.

"It is only because the grace of my guru, Swamidev, that I am here today. He saw potential in me and nurtured it. He sent me to America to teach in 1975 when I was only twenty-five years old. Jai, Jai, Sadhguru Swamidev!" Yogi Krishna Soham shouted as he lifted his hands to the sky. "Glory to the great guru."

Then he laughed heartily and turned his attention back to the group.

"It was Swamidev who gave me the name Krishna Soham the day when I was reborn, the day when he initiated me. He told me to spread the message of yoga," he said, then whispered softly, "Jai, Jai, Sadhguru Swamidev."

He combed through his beard with long, dark, well-manicured fingers.

"But, why Soham?" he asked the group. "Why So Hum? Do you know?"

The group was silent. Most shook their heads.

"For the auspicious reason that Soham means, I am that. My name represents the essence of yoga."

The students reached for their notebooks and started writing.

"No writing!" Yogi Krishna Soham commanded forcefully.

Shocked, everyone in the group dropped their notebooks.

"There is plenty of time to write," he added, in a soft voice with a smile. "You can write during every other lecture. For now, listen."

Somewhat baffled, the group complied.

"So Hum. I am that," he continued with cheerful animation. "That what?"

Again, his question was met with silence.

"That which does not change," he explained, acting like he was unraveling a whodunit mystery. "That was the great discovery of the rishis, the spiritual seers. They realized that if one sat long enough and peered into one's own being, then one could uncover a constant element. Unlike the body, emotions, and mind, it did not change."

Yogi Krishna Soham paused for effect.

"After making this realization, the rishis gathered for Satsangs — gatherings of truth — and compared their experiences with each other. Through their conversations, the rishis realized that those who had spent enough time in the state of meditation all shared the same experience. They had all uncovered that which does not change. They concluded that ultimate reality must be that, for the simple reason that it does not change."

Yogi Krishna Soham stared into the void above his students,

peering into eternity.

"Soham. So Hum," he whispered poetically. "I am that. I am that."

He snapped out of his trance and turned his attention back to the students.

"This realization—we don't have an exact date for when it happened, although most scholars agree that it was approximately five thousand years ago—represents the birth of yoga. In yoga, we yoke together, unify with, or uncover, that which does not change."

Most of the sixteen students were leaning forward, hanging on every word that Yogi Krishna Soham said. He was charismatic. There was no denying that.

"Another name for that which does not change is Atman. It is the name given to the essence in individuals. Another name was given to the essence of the universe, Brahman. One can imagine Brahman as the ocean and Atman as the drop. Both are qualitatively the same. Zero is infinity and infinity is zero. Yet, in Western society, Atman has also been given other names, such as the soul, the self, the witness, and the I-I. Do you understand?"

Without waiting for a reply, Yogi Krishna Soham continued.

"Of course, you don't," he declared joyfully. "Understanding that which does not change is experiential, not mental or philosophical. You cannot understand it through talking or thinking. No. The only way is direct experience, through the practice of yoga."

The students looked stunned. To his credit, Yogi Krishna Soham picked up on that.

"Think of it this way," he said. "You can only know the taste of chocolate through your taste buds, correct? No lecture can ever explain the taste of chocolate. Only experience will do."

A few of the students nodded their heads in agreement.

"The same is true with that which does not change. Only experience will do."

Most of the students still looked baffled.

"Let's back up," he proposed. "The rishis made a stunning

realization. They realized that, at the core of their being, there was a consciousness that did not change, which provided them with bliss, a feeling of unconditional happiness. They wanted to share this realization with the world. Imagine the urgency they must have felt," he continued. "For them, it must have been like when you taste a new kind of food or hear a fantastic song, and you want to share that experience with the world, you want to shout it from the rooftops. That's what it must have been like. They must have wanted to share their discovery with everyone. It wasn't quite that simple, however, because that which does not change had no references in language at that time. Therefore, they created new words, ideas, and philosophies to explain that which does not change to human beings who had not yet experienced the spiritual connection firsthand, but even that wasn't enough."

He shook his head for dramatic effect.

"No, because as soon as the rishis started telling others about their experiences, started making an effort to teach them how to experience it for themselves, they realized that the ever-changing nature of the mind would be the biggest obstacle. Disturbances in the mind cover that which does not change like clouds cover the sun. To transmit their firsthand knowledge, they had to create yoga, the path of practice and experience."

Many in the audience gasped for air like they had been holding their breath.

"It's okay," Yogi Krishna Soham responded with a smile on his face. "You don't need to get all of this today. I just wanted to go over the basics, so that you understand where the practices come from."

The group let out a collective sigh of relief.

"Here is what you need to know," he said with gusto. "Yoga is at least three things. First, yoga is an experiential state of union. Second, yoga is the philosophy that explains that which does not change. Third—and most importantly for the purposes of this yoga teacher training—yoga is a family of practices, which includes postures, breathing, relaxation, mental attitudes, and meditation techniques, that are meant to help the practitioner uncover that which does not change. You understand? Yes?"

Several people were nodding.

"How then did we end up with seemingly different paths of yoga?" he continued.

It was a rhetorical question that no one attempted to answer.

"The rishis created paths that were supported by natural tendencies. They realized that human beings were—and still are—mostly driven by three things, namely action, emotion, and intellect."

Yogi Krishna Soham repeated these three words with energy, using physical gestures to underscore them. When he said action, he showed his hands, when he said emotion, he pointed to his heart, and when he said intellect, he tapped on his head.

"In their wisdom," he continued, "the rishis noticed that people, although influenced by all three, had a predominant mode of operation and could be categorized as mostly active, emotional or intellectual. Their primary objective was to teach people how to uncover that which does not change, but—and this is the pure genius of it—instead of trying to teach their techniques in a way that they, themselves, liked to learn in, the rishis approached people where they were. That is how the four major paths of yoga were born."

Yogi Krishna Soham remained in a perfect lotus pose. His eyes sparkled, and his smooth face radiated energy as he continued to explain the fundamentals of yoga to this group of would-be yoga teachers.

"For active persons, the rishis created the path of Karma Yoga," he explained, "which is the path of non-attachment. Instead of focusing on the outcome, the Karma Yogi sees action as its own reward. By dwelling firmly in the present moment and detaching himself from the results of his actions, he uncovers that which does not change. Karma Yoga," he said and raised his hands to emphasize the physical connection, "is the yoga of action."

A few of the students mouthed the words silently, the yoga of action.

"For emotional persons," he said, placing both hands over his heart, "the rishis created the path of Bhakti Yoga. Through prayers, chanting and ceremonies, the practitioner is lifted out of emotions of darkness, anger, fear, and despair, into loftier emotions of love, empathy, and compassion. When dwelling in those altruistic emotions, that which does not change is uncovered. Therefore, Bhakti Yoga is the yoga of divine emotion."

Mimicking the master, several students held their hearts and mouthed the words, the yoga of divine emotion.

"For rational persons, the rishis created the path of Jnana Yoga, where the intellect is used as a scalpel to remove illusions. The Jnana Yogi uses the mantra, neti-neti, which means, not this-not that, to identify everything that changes, thusly uncovering what is left, the unchanging nature of Atman. It is an exclusionary method. By uncovering that which is not, you uncover what is. The body changes, neti-neti, then it is not the Atman. The mind changes, neti-neti, then it is not Atman, and so on, until nothing's left except that which does not change. Jnana yoga," Yogi Krishna Soham said, pointing to his head, "is the yoga of intellectual discernment."

Several people in the room raised their hands, wanting to ask questions, but Yogi Krishna Soham ignored them and kept on talking.

"You must be thinking," he said, "Yogi Krishna, you are not describing the yoga I know today. Where are the postures, the breathing techniques, and the meditation? For all of that, we have the path of Raja Yoga. Raja means emperor or king, the highest form a human being could take in the days when yoga was born. Raja Yoga means the highest or supreme yoga. It includes ethics, postures, breathing techniques, sensory withdrawal, concentration, and meditation. From Raja Yoga comes Hatha Yoga, the yoga of energy balance, from which are derived the yoga postures that many call yoga in the West today. The Raja Yogi devotes his life to the practice of yoga and through systematic effort he unveils—"

"—that which does not change," the group responded, after a brief moment of silence when Yogi Krishna Soham did not complete his own sentence.

"Good! You were listening," he said with a big grin on his face. "Unveiling that which does not change is the central objective of yoga. In fact, you can measure whether or not something is yoga by asking a simple question. Does the practice help me unveil that which does not change or is it covering that which does not change? For example, without proper attitude, yoga postures can easily lead to a narcissistic attachment to the body. The body is constantly changing, and an attachment to it does not help one reveal the underlying reality. Therefore, if practiced with an attitude of attachment to health, strength or flexibility, the postures are no longer yoga, but rather an exercise in narcissism and vanity. Only when the positions are used as a means to an end—practiced to prepare the body for meditation—are they an integral part of real yoga. Intention matters. When you are in doubt, you can apply the test. Ask, does the practice help me or keep me from unveiling that which does not change? If your answer is that it helps, then it is yoga, if it hinders, then it is not yoga."

One of the women in the class had been holding up her hand for several minutes while the others had given up.

"Yes?" Yogi Krishna Soham finally asked, nodding in her direction.

"Mister Yogi Krishna Soham," she said. "My name is Valentina Bosetti. I am an Anusara Yoga teacher, and I did not hear you mention any of the yoga paths that I know and love. You say there are only four yoga paths, but what about Ashtanga Yoga, Bikram Yoga, Sivananda Yoga, and Kripalu Yoga? Aren't these just as important as the other paths you just described?"

In the blink of an eye, Yogi Krishna Soham's demeanor changed, his brow sunk and he became serious, angry even.

"Young lady. Your question represents everything that is wrong with yoga today," he replied sternly. "People don't know the ABC of yoga. They don't understand where yoga comes from. They don't understand how human nature inspired three of the four primary paths. They don't understand that the path of Raja Yoga contains it all, the postures, breathing techniques and meditation methods. Today, these practices have been cut up, blended, and presented as separate paths. What you speak of is trademark yoga, created for marketing purposes in the West. Even Hatha Yoga, the original physical path, is derived from Raja Yoga. There are only four primary paths."

"But—"

"No!" Yogi Krishna Soham thundered. "Your question is stupid, miss Bosetti, a symptom of the corrupt fitness yoga in the West."

The atmosphere in the room soured. Even those who had hung on his every word during the introduction were taken aback by Yogi Krishna Soham's admonition. Valentina was almost brought to tears by his response.

"Even if I cannot correct every misunderstanding," Yogi Krishna Soham continued, oblivious to her emotional sensitivity, "I need to rectify it immediately when I hear such an utterly false impression being set forth in my ashram."

The yoga master seemed genuinely angry for a few moments, but then, in the blink of an eye — like a father who scolds his child, but is not affected himself — he regained his cheerful and charismatic disposition.

"Dear students. I can promise you this," he then added with a broad smile. "After you have been through my yoga teacher training, you will understand the ABC of yoga. You will understand the fundamentals of posture, breathing, meditation, and philosophy. You will be well versed in traditional Hatha Yoga. And if you choose to do so, you will be able to teach any form of trademark yoga you like — but," he added, "you will be able to do so with complete understanding of real yoga."

Govinda entered the back of the room and motioned to his guru, signaling that the lecture was nearly over.

"There are only four major paths of yoga," Yogi Krishna Soham concluded calmly, leaning back on his hands and releasing his legs from the lotus pose. "Never forget that. Three are based on human psychology, and one is a compilation of techniques. The goal of each of the paths remains the same — to unveil that which does not change. The four paths are like four sides of a pyramid. All lead to the same pinnacle." He put his hands in prayer position. "Namaste!" he said, bowed, then stood up and left.

Govinda stood at the front of the room, next to the stage.

"Okay guys," he said, "let's take a five-minute break." He looked behind him to see if Yogi Krishna Soham was gone, then added in a lower than usual tone. "Gurudev does not tolerate emotional sensitivity in his class. He is old school. His guru admonished him many times when he was younger, and he has a tendency to do the same. Please understand that it comes from a place of caring and love. He wants to break through your ego and your misapprehensions so your Atman can shine through."

Chapter Three

After a break that was ten minutes longer than announced, everyone gathered in the yoga hall for introductions. Per Govinda's instructions, the sixteen students now sat in a semicircle.

Govinda was sitting in full lotus pose to the right of the stage. He bowed his head to the floor when Yogi Krishna Soham entered the room and stayed that way until his guru was seated. Several of the teacher trainees followed suit and bowed their heads, while a larger part of the group looked on, uncertain how to behave.

"Okay guys," Govinda said, after getting a nod of approval from Yogi Krishna Soham. "It's time for introductions. Please state your name, tell us a little bit about yourself, and tell us why you decided to attend this yoga teacher training. We will go clockwise, starting on the left side of the stage. Edna, if you would begin."

"Me?" a brown haired, athletic woman answered. She was wearing green hemp pants and a white v-neck blouse.

"Yes, if you don't mind," Govinda replied.

"Okay," she responded, hesitating slightly before she continued. "My name is Edna Ginsberg. I am thirty-three. I work as a lawyer in New Jersey, where I live with my husband Paul, who is also a lawyer. Please, spare me the lawyer jokes. I know them all."

A few of the students giggled, evidently reminded of lawyer jokes.

"I have been to the ashram two times before," Edna proceeded to explain, "and know Yogi Krishna to be an excellent teacher. When he suggested that I take his yoga teacher training, I jumped at the opportunity. I am trying to bring an ethical standard, peace of mind, and one-pointed focus to my work. So far, yoga has helped me with all of that and more. I hope that this training will allow me to delve deeper. I am here for the five hundred hour training."

"You are most welcome to this program, miss Edna," Yogi

Krishna Soham responded. "We need more ethical lawyers."

"Namaste, Yogi," she replied, placing her hands in prayer pose and bowing slightly.

"Namaste!" he responded.

"Next," Govinda exclaimed, evidently wanting to keep the procession going.

"Hello everyone," a soft-featured creature with a round face and curly, shoulder-length hair said in a muted voice. "My name is Blossom. I guess I am the youngest in the group. I turned nineteen earlier this summer. I was raised by a single father in California. From when I can remember, we always practiced yoga after he came home from work. We own every single DVD that Yogi Krishna Soham ever produced and have played them over and over again. I am so excited to be here. I wish I could stay for the five hundred hour program. It looks so wonderful. Maybe next time. I look forward to learning from all of you."

"Welcome, miss Blossom," Yogi Krishna Soham responded.

"Thank you," she answered, blushing a little from the attention she was receiving.

Next, three women in their early twenties introduced themselves. Camille Lundgren was a blonde graduate student from Sweden. The other two were recently graduated veterinarians from Germany, Gerwalta Brun and Malin Holzer, who had met Yogi Krishna Soham two years earlier when he had traveled to Cologne to teach.

"My name is Thomas Dunlop," a cleanly shaven, bald, and rather stocky man with a black goatee said before Govinda could prompt him. He was dressed in a black t-shirt and black shorts. "I am twenty-nine years old and have been teaching yoga for the past five years. I own a small studio in the town of Evergreen in Colorado where I live with my wife Penny and our three-year-old son Charles, who, by the way, has never had sugar."

His statement prompted oohs, aahs, good for yous, and one, I wish more people would do that.

"And why are you here, Thomas?" Govinda asked, his accent seemingly thicker than before.

"Well," Thomas replied, "I learned how to teach yoga from Yogi Vasudev in Colorado. He is an authentic teacher with a small practice, but he has never bothered to register with Yoga Alliance. Seeing as I have a studio now, I want to start offering a yoga teacher training, and for that, I feel like I need the five hundred hour credentials that this program provides. I am steeped in my own practice, but I come here with an open mind, ready to learn about yoga from a new perspective. I already gained a lot from your earlier lecture, Yogi Krishna Soham," he said, turning his attention directly to the yoga master. "I liked how you simplified the paths of Bhakti, Jnana, and Karma Yoga by connecting them to human psychology and needs. I look forward to learning more from you, sir."

Yogi Krishna Soham looked pleased. "What kind of yoga do you teach at your studio, mister Thomas?" he asked with a smile.

"That's a trick question, isn't it, sir?" Thomas replied. "I teach traditional Hatha Yoga, focusing on the practical benefits for different groups of people. For example, I offer a four-week program for beginners and an eight-week program for stiff and stressed men. Over the past two years, I have increased male participation from ten percent to almost forty percent."

That statement drew additional oohs and aahs. Thomas was being well received.

"Good," Yogi Krishna Soham replied, adding, "did you know that Vasudev is also a name for Krishna?"

"Yes sir, I did," Thomas replied.

"For those of you who do not know, all the pictures on the walls — except for the one of Swamidev — are of Krishna, the sustaining aspect of God. My birth name was Gopal, which is a name for Krishna. Govinda is another name for Krishna and so is Vasudev. We are surrounded by Krishna. That is auspicious indeed. Welcome, mister Thomas. Give my regards to your guru."

Before Thomas could answer and say that he did not consider

Yogi Vasudev to be his guru, Govinda prompted the next person in line.

Stacey Garrick-Tien introduced herself and her husband, the Asian American Ang Lin Tien. The two of them were in their late twenties, newly married, and were at the ashram for the two hundred hour training. They were a peculiar couple. She was sickly white, skin and bones thin, with large facial features, and was at least six inches taller than him. He was about five-foot-two and had a round face, which made his head look like a full moon, thanks in part to his buzz cut. He wore rectangular glasses, a blue tank top, and baggy purple pants.

Next in line was the woman who had been admonished by Yogi Krishna Soham in the previous session. She put on a brave face, smiled, and made her introduction.

"My name is Valentina Bosetti," she said, looking at the group rather than at the stage. "I am a Scorpio, a retired professional ballet dancer, and a certified Anusara yoga teacher. Because of my question earlier, I must say that even though Anusara is not one of the four primary paths of yoga, it is a growing brand that I am proud to be associated with. Your program," she said, now talking directly to Yogi Krishna Soham, "was recommended to me by a friend who is also an Anusara teacher. She said that it was the most authentic program she had attended."

Valentina was by far the most beautiful woman in the program. She looked to be in her mid-thirties, had flowing, shoulder-length, brown hair, green eyes, a small nose, full lips and her body was strong, athletic, and graceful from years and years of training. She looked around the room as she finished her introduction.

"I look forward to getting to know all of you. I am very spiritual. I have learned Reiki and astrology, and would love to read your stars or give you a healing session in between classes."

Several people in the room said thank you and Namaste.

It looked like Yogi Krishna Soham was about to respond to Valentina's introduction, but Govinda was quick to prompt the next person in line.

"Jasmine, why don't you go next?"

"Yes," responded a Latino woman in her early twenties, wearing a short tank top and tight black leggings, her midsection exposed. "Me llamo Jasmine," she said in a thick accent. "I am a belly dancer. I perform and teach belly dancing in Miami. I come from Chile, and I love, love, love hot yoga. I go to classes five times a week. I want to learn how to teach yoga, and this is the shortest program I found. Two hundred hours in two weeks. I love it."

"That's why I chose this program as well," said the woman next to her, assuming that Jasmine was done. "Hi! I am Poppy Williams, and I am an aerobics teacher."

She looked the part, with bleached blonde hair, an excessive tan, a big smile, and a peppy personality.

"I came here because it is the quickest way to achieve the five hundred hour certification. I am turning fifty in three years, and I want to get ready for the second half of my teaching career — you know, slow it down a little bit. I have mostly done hot yoga and power yoga over the years, but I look forward to learning more about traditional Hatha Yoga. I go running every day, so, if anyone wants to join me, let me know in between classes. I look forward to learning from you, Yogi."

"Thank you, miss Poppy," Yogi Krishna Soham responded.

After that, three women introduced themselves.

First, Laurie Sanders, a twenty-four-year-old, who was raised on a cattle farm in Texas and was majoring in journalism at UT in Austin. Yoga was her preferred exercise method, and she wanted to be certified at the highest level, said this was the best way she could find to spend her summer.

Second, the oldest woman in the group, Betsy Brigham, a self-proclaimed Christian lady with curly gray hair and glasses. She was nearing retirement and wanted to complete the two hundred hour certification to support her personal practice, said she would in all likelihood not teach.

Third, was Andrea Courson, a chubby elementary school teacher in her early fifties, who was doing the five hundred hour training and wanted to learn how to teach yoga to kids.

The circle was almost complete. Only two men remained. BJ went first.

"My name is Bjarni Jóhann Helgason, and I am from Iceland," he said, pronouncing his name harshly to make sure that no one could replicate it, "but all of you can call me BJ or guy from Iceland if you can't remember my name. I am forty-six, a full-time investor and a marathon runner. My girlfriend Sara and I are planning to open a yoga studio next year, and I pride myself on knowing everything I can about my investments before I take the plunge. That is why I am here. To prepare for my investment."

"Welcome, mister Bjarni," Yogi Krishna Soham replied with a surprisingly accurate pronunciation.

"Thank you, Yogi Krishna. May I call you that?"

"Yes. You may call me Yogi Krishna, Yogi Soham, or just Yogi. That goes for all of you," he added with a laugh, "although Gurudev is reserved for my disciples. At the end of the day, though, names are only labels. That is one reason why we take spiritual names. To shed labels."

"Thank you, Yogi," BJ said again.

"Last one guys, then we take a break," Govinda said.

"Greetings all," a five-foot-four, curly haired, big-nosed man with thick rimmed black glasses said. "My name is Kurt Adler. I am thirty-seven and a practicing psychologist. I have been married to my wife Bea for two years, which incidentally is also how long I have been a vegan. Loving it. Feel better than I have felt in years. I came to this yoga teacher training because I want to add meditation, yoga, and relaxation to my therapy practice. Most emotional problems my patients are dealing with are stress related. If they could learn how to reduce their stress levels, even just a little, my job would become much easier and more productive."

"Yoga is extremely effective for tension relief," Yogi Krishna

Soham replied. "I am glad you are with us, mister Kurt. Welcome."

"Thank you, Yogi Krishna," Kurt replied.

"Okay, guys. That's it for this session," Govinda said. "We break now for dinner and then we have Satsang tonight where Gurudev will talk about the purpose of Hatha Yoga."

Chapter Four

"This must be the strangest way in which I have spent a Saturday night in ages," BJ said to his roommates. "I'm usually out with friends or at least watching a movie. Never would I have imagined that I'd be sitting in a room with two other men at ten o'clock in the evening, getting ready for bed."

The three of them, Kurt, Thomas, and BJ, were tuckered after their first half-day of classes at the ashram. Thomas was lying on his back in the top bunk, while Kurt and BJ were both in their respective bottom bunks. Ang Lin was nowhere to be seen, probably out with his wife, Stacey. The couple had brought their car all the way from Portland.

"I must admit that this is calmer than usual, even for me," Thomas said, as he watched the ceiling fan rotate above him.

The door to stood ajar. An increasing sound of chatter came from the seating area where many of the women had gathered. Crickets could also be heard chirping outside the bedroom window. The AC, which, in accordance with the ashram power saving protocols, had only been turned on when all the teacher trainees arrived earlier that day, and now it kept the room comfortable.

"You know what I don't get, BJ?" Kurt said, breaking the thoughtful silence. "Why invest in a yoga studio? It doesn't sound like the most profitable way to put your money to work."

"That's a strange question," BJ replied, "coming from a man at a yoga teacher training."

"Don't get me wrong," Kurt answered, "I understand the idea of running a yoga studio, but it doesn't sound like a profitable investment, especially not for a man who primarily invests in real estate."

"I get that," BJ replied as he sat up and placed his elbows on his thighs so he could look over at Kurt. "At first, it was because of my girlfriend, Sara. She recently turned thirty, loves yoga, and I wanted to support her. However, when I started doing the math, I realized that yoga could also be good business. Maybe not great, but good, which reminds me," he continued, looking up at Thomas, "how is your studio in Colorado doing?"

"I'd love to tell you nothing but good news," Thomas replied as he also sat up and leaned his back against the wall, "but I have to admit that it's been tough. There are many yoga teachers and yoga studios to compete with. I have found a way to make it work, but only to make ends meet. I mostly make money from open classes and series — you know, yoga for beginners and yoga for stiff and stressed men — but the main reason I am here is so that I can offer a yoga teacher training of my own. That's where the real money is."

"Don't you think that the market is becoming saturated?" Kurt asked, turning his head to see Thomas above him.

"I hope not. Based on all my calculations, the yoga teacher training I plan to offer should become the financial cornerstone of my studio."

"But, aren't you running yourself out of business?" BJ asked. "I mean, there isn't going to be an endless supply of students for the yoga teachers everyone is churning out, is there?"

"Hopefully, interest will increase. We still haven't reached critical mass. Yes, yoga is popular, but it's not as mainstream as it can be. I am banking on it — literally."

Kurt stood up and closed the door to the hallway. He then returned to his bottom bunk and sat down.

"What do you guys think of this teacher training so far?" he asked.

"I think it shows promise," Thomas replied, his voice sounding optimistic. "I was especially happy with tonight's lecture on Hatha Yoga, with how Yogi Krishna talked about the need for balance, how strong and stiff people need flexibility while limber people need to firm up, how people with fast paced energy need to experiment with slower movement and vice versa."

"Really? You think it shows promise? Me, I am confused," BJ added after a short pause. "I don't know what to make of this program, especially the two teachers."

"What do you mean?" Kurt inquired.

"I mean, Govinda and Yogi Krishna are special characters, aren't they? One minute they are giving great advice, inspiring lectures, the other, well, they're just rude—"

"It's not that bad," Thomas interrupted.

"Not that bad?" BJ responded. "Did you see what happened today? You're the psychologist Kurt, what do you think?"

"There are definitely some interesting dynamics going on. Govinda defers entirely to the authority of his guru but tries to mimic him when left in charge. Yogi Krishna Soham is a harder nut to crack. He is knowledgeable—I'll give him that—but he seems to swing from being extremely likable and charismatic to being authoritarian and controlling."

"That's just the Indian way of teaching," Thomas said as he climbed down from his top bunk and sat down up against the wall by the window. He looked masculine in his black tank top, guns blazing and shoulders bulging, not at all the usual yoga physique.

"I have studied with Yogi Vasudev for years," he explained, "and have, in addition to that, taken several courses with Indian yogis. They all show similar authoritarian traits, although maybe not as pronounced as what we have seen here. Do you remember how teachers in the West used to be strict and hand out corporal punishment?"

"How could I forget," Kurt replied. "I was at the receiving end of several spankings in my youth, and even today, at private schools, some teachers still do that."

"Well, the Indian system of teaching is still very strict, although they usually don't hand out beatings. Their way of instructing is patriarchal. The guru is in the role of the father or supreme authority, and he administers chidings anytime he sees fit. In the West, we have in most cases developed more refined and balanced methods of teaching, but that's not how it's done within the Indian spiritual community — not yet, anyway."

"I don't know if I can handle that," BJ said and shook his head. "I mean, I am forty-six years old, and as I told Kurt earlier, I am in no mood to be treated like a child, scolded by a wannabe guru and a spiritual father figure."

"It's not as horrible as it sounds," Thomas replied. "Once you know about this — their tendency to teach with authority — you can look past it. I am sure that aside from the occasional scolding, Yogi Krishna is an excellent teacher, at least, that's what his books imply."

"That much is true," Kurt interjected. "His books are fairly well written and to the point. I'll even admit that his teaching today, about that which does not change and the four major paths of yoga, was illuminating. For a psychologist, like myself, it was interesting to see how core psychological traits and characteristics influenced both yoga philosophy and teaching methods. Based on what he said, it is evident that psychology is a much older profession than some would have us believe."

"So what? Are you saying that just because he is potentially a good teacher we should overlook his ways of reprimanding people?" BJ asked, lifting his hands in protest. "He nearly brought a woman to tears today."

"I guess the answer to that question depends on how you want to spend the next five weeks," Kurt responded. "Do you want to make enemies of Yogi Krishna Soham and Govinda — although it may be too late with Govinda, you seem to have gotten on his nerves already," he said with a chuckle, " — or do you want to enjoy your time here and get along?"

"I guess I'd rather get along," BJ said.

"Plus," Kurt added, "you have to admit that Valentina was overly sensitive this afternoon — as most people are these days — so you can't really say that Yogi Krishna nearly brought her to tears. You can say that she almost brought herself to tears. Yogi Krishna wasn't that harsh in his admonition."

"Whatever her reaction, Yogi Krishna Soham was correct in what he said," Thomas extrapolated. "The question, what kind of yoga do you teach, only refers to brands of physical yoga, not the four primary paths of real yoga, paths that help the practitioner uncover that which does not change. What he said was all right, but how he said it, well, I can't say I was happy with that, but I can't say I was surprised either."

"Again, do the two of you think that we should just be okay with that kind of behavior?" BJ asked, clearly not happy.

"Shouldn't we at least give this program a chance?" Thomas asked and jumped up off the floor where he'd been sitting. "Maybe we shouldn't judge this whole program, or those two men, based on first impressions. We've only known them for one day. Let's have this discussion again in a week or so. By then we should have a clearer picture of what they are actually like."

Kurt and BJ looked at the younger man.

"You're kind of smart for your age," Kurt replied. "Not even thirty yet and already you have a knack for diplomacy."

"You're right," BJ added with a sigh. "I guess we should give them the benefit of the doubt,"

"I want to get everything I can out of this program," Thomas said, "and quite frankly, I don't see how focusing on the teacher's faults will help me do that. Now, if you'll excuse me, I need to go to the bathroom and get ready for bed."

"The young gun has a point," Kurt said after Thomas left the room.

"Yeah. We should probably give this program a chance."

"So," Kurt continued after a brief silence. "You have a thirty-year-old girlfriend, huh? Is she hot like Jasmine and Valentina?"

"Is my girlfriend hot?" BJ answered with a bewildered laugh. "Are you sure you are a psychologist, Kurt?"

Chapter Five

Gong. Gong. Gong.

That was it, the sound of waking up at the ashram. It was five-thirty in the morning, and there was no snooze button. Never in his life had BJ woken up this early, except maybe to catch a flight. Back in Iceland, waking up at seven was considered early.

Judging from their activity, both Kurt and Thomas were A-types, up and running within a minute, but Ang Lin, who bunked above BJ, didn't move a muscle. He had come into the room after his roommates had gone to sleep the previous night. None of the men knew when.

BJ got dressed, walked to the outhouses in the dark, brushed his teeth to the sound of insects, washed his face, and emptied his bladder. Several of the women were already showering in the stalls behind the toilets. Many seemed to have woken up before the bell rung. BJ noticed a sizable wasp nest in the ceiling above the bathroom mirror. The wasps looked to be busy, flying in and out through a gap between the corrugated metal roofing and the wooden frame that held up the structure. To his relief, the wasps left him alone, but, as he stood there, repeated shivers went up and down his spine.

When he was done, BJ returned his toiletries to his room, said good morning to Ang Lin, who was just getting up, and headed for the yoga hall. He entered the room just before six. Most of the students were already there, whispering, the sounds creating a muted symphony of chatters. Yogi Krishna Soham was sitting on the stage in full lotus pose, already in what seemed like a deep state of meditation. When Govinda entered the room, with Ang Lin on his heels, he made shushing noises several times until the group quieted down.

BJ's back was stiff, and his legs wouldn't bend the way they usually did later in the day. He decided to sit with cross-legged with his back up against the wall, situated midway between the entrance and the stage, to the left of Yogi Krishna Soham.

Govinda struck a large copper Tibetan Bowl six times when a clock on the wall in the back of the room turned six, signifying the start of meditation. The students looked to the stage and waited for guidance with their eyes open, but no directions were given. When they realized that they wouldn't be getting any assistance, those who had no prior meditation experience tried to mimic what they were seeing their teacher do on stage. For the next half-hour, the room was restless. People were constantly shifting positions, opening and closing their eyes, waiting for the session to be over.

Finally, at six-thirty, Yogi Krishna opened his eyes. BJ couldn't wait for the sitting part to be over, his butt cheeks had gone to sleep several times and felt numb, but, to his chagrin, it was time for breathing exercises, so the sitting continued.

Yogi Krishna Soham guided the group through several rounds of cleansing breath, called Kapalbhati, and then moved on to alternate nostril breathing, called Anuloma Viloma. Breathing through one nostril at a time was surprisingly strenuous. BJ found himself stopping in between rounds to catch his breath, probably because of the restricted airflow through his right nostril. He'd never realized there could be so much difference between sides.

It was almost seven when the students were invited to stand up and roll out their yoga mats. Most everyone grunted as they shook off the morning stiffness. Sitting for an hour had taken a toll.

The yoga routine started with vigorous sun salutations—so vigorous, in fact, that within a few minutes half the people in the room were huffing and puffing. Yogi Krishna Soham flowed gracefully and seemingly without effort from one movement to another. The sun salutations continued for thirty minutes, with multiple variations that BJ had never done before. Then came headstand preparations, a familiar shoulderstand routine, forward bends, backward bends, and twists, all lead seamlessly by the aging yoga master who had a laconic approach, using the fewest number of words possible to instruct.

Bend forward. Stretch. Stand on one leg like a tree. That was how Yogi Krishna taught his students. His class was void of poetry — void of the spiritual and emotional language that had become so pervasive in Westernized yoga. His teaching method was simple, elegant, to the point, effective, and challenging, much harder than BJ had expected, especially considering Yogi Krishna Soham's age.

If I can do half of what he can do when I am sixty-five, BJ repeatedly thought during the class, then I will be more than happy.

BJ's well-trained marathon muscles shook and burned as he put maximum effort into every pose. That was his way of doing things, with maximum effort.

When the posture session came to an end, everyone was sweating. Even the dancer Valentina and the aerobics teacher Poppy had sweat stained hairlines. Relaxation was a welcome relief, yet BJ could hear stomachs growling as Yogi Krishna Soham led the group through a progressive muscle relaxation technique. No one had eaten yet.

When the morning practice was over, a few minutes after eight, BJ ran to the kitchen as hungry as he'd ever been. There, Lilavati had prepared oatmeal with raisins and flax seeds seasoned with cinnamon and cloves. She was humming along with Indian devotional music coming from her small radio. BJ acknowledged her with a bow and grabbed a full bowl of oatmeal, several grapes, and a banana. To his immense relief, coffee was served. He'd been afraid that he would have to go without that during his stay and suffer the withdrawal symptoms. He sat on the floor at the table closest to the entrance and began devouring his food.

Govinda came into the room, bent down beside him and said: "Good morning, Bjarni. It's good to be hungry, isn't it?"

BJ nodded and kept munching.

"After I first came here," Govinda said with a friendly smile, "I realized that I hadn't really been hungry for years. I had always eaten just because it was time to eat. Now, I look forward to being hungry because each bite tastes sweeter when true hunger leads to eating."

BJ nodded again. Govinda patted him on the back and got in line.

"What was that about?" Kurt asked as he sat down next to BJ.

"He was talking about hunger," BJ answered with his mouth full. "He's right. It feels great to be hungry."

"He want's to be your friend," Kurt replied with a smirk, now also digging into his bowl with a spoon.

The two men ate quietly.

"I have to admit that Yogi Krishna surprised me this morning," BJ said after he finished his bowl of oatmeal, now sitting up against the wall behind Kurt with a cup of coffee in hand, enjoying every sip.

"How so?" Kurt asked.

The two of them were alone at their table. Groups were already forming among the students.

"For one, I didn't think that the class would be this hard, both because of his age and because of his spiritual inclinations. I thought we would be practicing the yoga poses slowly and with awareness. It was quite a workout. If we are going to be doing this twice a day for five weeks, I can't wait to see the results."

"Results? You don't have much weight to lose my friend," Kurt replied, "unlike Thomas and me. Both of us could lose a few pounds without regret."

"I am not thinking about pounds, just my form, and flexibility. I have always been rather stiff, and my running routine hasn't helped. I'm thinking about taking a break from the running while I am here and focus entirely on the yoga." BJ continued as Kurt took a seat next to him up against the wall. "Sitting on the floor is what's going to kill me, though. My knees, buttocks, hips, and back, are not agreeing with that at all, and it's only day two."

"Agreed. I would do almost anything for a chair. There must be some way of doing this more comfortably," Kurt replied.

"I asked Govinda, and he just told me to get more pillows and blankets. Stack them up as high as you need to, we have plenty, he said."

"I told you. He wants to be your friend. He must sense that the two of you got off on the wrong foot."

"I guess. He's okay."

"Did you see the hotties stretching during class?" Kurt whispered, leaning closer.

"Come on, Kurt. It's not even nine o'clock."

"Give me some leeway here, BJ. I am not used to being surrounded by beautiful women."

"Well, you're going to have to get over it. Judging by what I have seen, this is what teaching yoga is going to be like. You'll mostly be teaching women, that is unless you start teaching to stiff and stressed men like Thomas."

"Then I guess I'll have to 'tame' my libido," Kurt said, making air quotes, sporting a sly smile.

"I am serious," BJ replied. "You can't teach yoga if you continually allow your mind to undress the students. How do you tame your libido during therapy sessions?"

"That's easy. The women who come there are fully dressed. In yoga class, it's all the spandex and cleavage. The outlines demand my attention."

"Well, I'll ask you not to drag me into your sexual fantasies. I am happy with my girlfriend now, and I look forward to opening a yoga studio with her in Iceland. I can't afford any distractions. I am training myself to look past sexuality in yoga classes."

"I may not have a thirty-year-old girlfriend, but it's not like I plan to cheat. I am married, remember? I simply believe that there is no harm in looking — but if you insist, I'll keep these 'impure' thoughts to myself," Kurt replied, still smiling. "I don't know how Yogi Krishna does it, surrounded by beautiful women all the time who hang on his every word."

BJ shrugged. Somehow, Yogi Krishna Soham seemed above all that.

The two men finished their coffee. Then they gathered their utensils and headed for the sink.

"Are you feeling better about your decision to come here?" Kurt asked as they walked towards the kitchen in the corner.

"As a matter of fact, I am. The class this morning was challenging, and I like to be kept on my toes. I can actually say that I look forward to what's coming next, you know, learning how to build poses from the ground up. How about you?"

"I feel the same. I think we may actually enjoy it here."

Chapter Six

"Hey! Guy from Iceland. Come, sit with us."

It was Andrea Courson, the fifty-something teacher from Boston, who called BJ as he was walking by, getting ready for bed. She was curled up in the dormitory seating area with Laurie, the journalism student and cowgirl from Texas, and Edna, the lawyer from New Jersey.

"Yeah, join us. Come over to the dark side," Laurie added playfully with dramatic effect.

"Okay," BJ said and sat down on a stack of colorful pillows, situating himself strategically across from the women, not knowing what he was getting himself into.

"Tell us about yourself, tall Icelandic man," Andrea said. "Married, kids, any deep dark secrets?"

"Not married, I have two kids, and no deep dark secrets," BJ replied with a smile.

"Come on. You're no fun," Laurie said. "At least tell us the names of your kids and how old they are."

"They are seven and eleven. My daughter is the younger one, and her name is Hulda. My son is older, and his name is Helgi."

"And their mom?" Andrea quizzed.

"Her name is Hafdís. We are no longer together."

"Divorced?" Edna chimed in.

"Nope, we never got married."

"Two kids and never got married," Andrea sounded out. "That's interesting. How long were you two together?"

"You ladies are very inquisitive," BJ replied, still smiling.

"We ask because you're an interesting man, mister guy from Iceland. We've never met anyone from Iceland before. We want to know all about you," Laurie said.

The three women were huddled together in the corner, while BJ maintained an appropriate distance.

"Okay, I'll humor you," he said after a short pause. "We were together for ten years."

"Ten years and you never got married? Is that common in Iceland?" Edna asked, her lawyer radar going up.

"It's pretty common. People move in together, have kids, then, if they are still together five or ten years down the road, maybe they get married."

"Are you telling us that Icelandic people think that marriage is more of a commitment than having kids? That's topsy-turvy," Andrea commented.

"I can't speak for all Icelandic people, but that was how I did it, except we never did get married," BJ replied, feeling slightly uncomfortable. "What about you ladies? Married, kids, deep dark secrets?"

"Not married, no kids — neither one on the radar," Laurie replied with the youthful and carefree attitude of a twenty-four-year-old.

"I am married, but we don't have any kids," Edna said, her voice not giving any indication of whether or not she was happily married.

"Never married, but I do have lots of kids," Andrea responded with pride. "My students are my kids. I adopt a new batch of twenty eager minds every year."

"What about deep dark secrets?" BJ inquired.

"We're not gonna tell you that. We just met," Andrea replied with a laugh.

"Shhh, we can't be too loud," Edna said in a low voice. "It's almost time for lights out."

"Yeah, but I'm not tired yet," Andrea whispered back. "Hey, BJ. You wanna hear some gossip?"

"Sure," BJ replied, shrugging his shoulders.

"Okay. Here is what we know so far," Andrea said. "Stacey and Ang Lin are having sex in their car, all the time, they may even be doing drugs, we don't know. We think that Jasmine may do more than belly dancing for a living, wink, wink, if you know what I mean, some stripping involved. Our peppy aerobics teacher Poppy spends an awful lot of her time in the top bunk and often looks like she's been crying, although she pretends not to show it, always wearing her fake smile. We haven't uncovered Valentina's deep dark secret yet, but no one can be so perfect, so beautiful, always wearing white, so eager to help others, there must be something there. The Swedish and German girls pretty much keep to themselves, and we haven't heard anything about old lady Betsy or young Blossom yet."

"Wow. You've been busy. We've only been here four days, and you already know all this. You should be an investigative journalist."

"I know. It's a gift," Andrea replied with a smile, "but we don't know anything about you guys yet. What can you tell us about Kurt and Thomas?"

"Not much, besides what they told everyone during orientation. We don't talk much about personal stuff. We discuss the program and ideas. It's a guy thing."

"Aww, come on, you've got to give us something," Laurie said, putting on her best display of puppy eyes.

"Sorry, ladies. No dirt from the boys quarters, except that we hardly ever see Ang Lin, and you've explained why. You really think that they are doing drugs?"

"At least once I detected the smell of weeds. Unmistakable," Laurie replied.

"Are you going to tell Yogi Krishna and Govinda? Stacey and Ang Lin could be dismissed from the program," BJ asked.

"We ain't no snitches," Andrea replied with attitude. "The gossip is just for fun. You see, with there being no TV or Internet, we are just engaging in old style facebooking."

"No, we won't tell," Edna confirmed. "Even if we had evidence, which we don't, I don't see how getting them into trouble would do anyone any good."

"Amen to that," Laurie said.

The group went momentarily quiet when Gerwalta, Malin, and Camille entered the building. The three foreigners acknowledged the gossip group in the corner, said goodnight and headed to their room.

"I just realized something," BJ said, breaking the silence. "All four of us are going to be in the five hundred hour training."

The ladies looked at each other with an expression of discovery.

"Yes, we are," Andrea said. "How do you like that? Four and a half more weeks together."

"Is it that long? I feel like we have already been here for ages," Laurie replied. "The days here are really long."

"Tell that to my body," Andrea said, grabbing flab and shaking it. "I knew I needed exercise, but this is far beyond what I expected. I have to take Ibuprofen every night just to be able to fall asleep."

"You're doing well, though," Laurie said. "You're very flexible."

"Don't kid a kidder kid," Andrea replied, putting on a serious face. "I know what I look like. I know that I don't fit the mold of a yoga lady, and I am fine with that. All I ask is that you don't patronize me with false praise. Praise me when I have made some real progress."

"Jeez. Sensitive," Laurie responded, putting her hands up in the air like she was backing off.

"How do you like the program so far?" Edna asked, changing the subject.

"I like it more every day," BJ replied. "I like learning about the postures, the breathing, and the anatomy, but I still haven't gotten a moment of peace during the meditation in the morning. My body just keeps screaming."

"Tell me about it," Andrea chimed in, "and they're not giving us any directions. What are we supposed to be doing?"

"Just focus on your breathing," Edna said. "It'll come. Yogi Krishna is teaching by example instead of giving directions. I was confused during the first program I attended here, but after a few days I settled down."

"It's probably easier when you can sit cross-legged without experiencing any pain," BJ said, shifting on the pillows to demonstrate how stiff his legs were.

"Yeah, I guess. Be patient, though, it'll come," Edna said with a smile, "just keep at it. I asked Govinda, and there will be a session on meditation next week. We will also devote more attention to it after the two hundred hour certification is done."

"That's good to hear," Laurie said with a sigh. "I have no trouble sitting. I just don't know what to do with my mind. I keep replaying episodes of my favorite TV shows and thinking about stuff that I shouldn't really be thinking about—you know," she said with a wink, "R-rated stuff."

"All my mind can think about is the pain I am experiencing," BJ said. "I hope it get's better. I figured I was in good shape when I came here, but the continual sitting on the floor—"

"It will get better," Govinda interrupted. He'd entered the room without them knowing about it. "When I first came here I couldn't sit for ten minutes. Now I can sit for an hour easily. You just have to break through the pain."

"Well, hello there Govinda. We didn't see you," Laurie said, putting on a big smile. "You wanna join us?"

"Sorry, guys. It's almost lights out time."

"Ahh, can't we stay up a little bit longer," Andrea said in a pleading baby voice.

"Five more minutes, then lights out," Govinda responded and walked up the stairs to his room.

"Thank you, Govinda," Andrea said, with her hands in prayer pose, bowing to him mockingly as he went out of sight.

"You need to give him a break, Andrea," Edna said. "He's just doing his job."

"Yeah, but he's just always bossing me around. That's my job," Andrea responded, "I'm the one who bosses people around."

"No, it's true," BJ said. "We need to give him a break. He's a good kid. It's a difficult task running this operation. He must sometimes feel like he is herding cats."

"Okay, okay," Andrea responded in a rare moment of solemnity. "I'll give him a break."

"Well, it was good to talk to you ladies," BJ said as he got up and yawned. "Lights out or not, I need to go to bed."

"Good night, guy from Iceland," the three women said in unison.

"Good night, ladies."

Chapter Seven

"Okay guys," Govinda said to Thomas and BJ, "we need to plant at least ten banana trees before our lunch break."

The three men were out in the midmorning sun. Temperatures were in the low nineties, and the humidity was well above eighty percent. They had only been in the field behind the ashram for a few minutes and were already sweating profusely in their t-shirts and shorts. BJ didn't want to stain his expensive running sneakers, so he wore flip-flops instead. His toes were already covered in dirt, as he was in charge of digging holes.

"I'm actually beginning to like this hour of service," BJ said to Thomas while Govinda wheelbarrowed a pile of dirt to an area nearby.

"Yeah," Thomas replied. "It's a nice break from all the learning and sitting."

"You're having trouble with sitting too?" BJ asked incredulously. "You, the yoga teacher?"

"I know, I didn't think I would, but I never sit on the floor this long at my studio or when I'm at home."

"Govinda says that it will get better. I hope he's right."

"I am sure he is. There are still entire societies that don't have chairs," Thomas said with a grin. "At least we know it's possible."

"Okay guys, here comes the tree," Govinda called out, as he carried a six-foot banana tree with his bare hands towards them. Thomas helped him guide the tree into place and together they pressured the dirt in around the base of the tree while BJ shoveled in a combination of compost and manure. The smell was horrible, made worse by the heat and humidity.

Once the tree was firmly in place, Govinda made sure that it was straight. He then took five large steps away from the tree, in line with the rest of what they had already planted that week, and declared:

"The next tree goes here."

BJ started digging and quickly filled the wheelbarrows again. As Govinda went to dump the dirt and pick up another tree, Thomas remarked: "You've got to hand it to Govinda. His work ethic is the best I've ever seen. He never takes a break from his duties, and even though he may seem harsh, I see him smile more often than not, performing each act stoically."

"Yeah. We were just talking about him last night, me and the three gossip girls, Andrea, Laurie, and Edna," BJ replied. "We shouldn't give him such a hard time. He is a good kid, doing a difficult job."

As if to underscore their point, Govinda was back before they knew it, returning with another tree. The three men repeated the progression, Thomas and Govinda holding the tree in place while BJ shoveled.

On their third tree of the day, BJ noticed critters crawling on Thomas's shoes.

"You have ants on your shoes, Thomas," BJ said.

Thomas looked down.

"Shit! Fire ants!" he cried.

Twenty large reddish ants were visible on Thomas's white sneakers.

"Quick! Wash them off with water," Govinda shouted.

In haste, Thomas took off. There was a hose nearby that the men had used to water the newly planted trees. Thomas picked it up and sprayed off the attacking ants in a few sweeping motions. He returned, feet soaking wet.

"Any bites?" Govinda asked.

"No. I don't think so," Thomas replied.

"Good. Fire ant bites really sting," Govinda said.

"Are they similar wasp bites?" BJ asked out of curiosity. There were no fire ants in Iceland.

"Worse," Govinda replied and then added, "you should really get some better shoes for yard work BJ. You are inviting insects to bite you in those open flip flops."

"Better shoes? Sure. But I don't know where I can purchase any. I found the strip mall you suggested, but there are no shoe stores there. Without Google Maps, I don't know where anything is around here."

"I'll look it up for you during lunch break," Govinda replied. "I have some work to do on the computer. If there is nothing nearby, you can probably hitch a ride with Lilavati next time she goes shopping for groceries."

"Thanks," BJ replied. "I appreciate that."

"No problem," Govinda said with a smile. "Now, enough with the chit-chat. We have seven trees to plant and forty minutes to do it. Back to work."

On they went. Dig, plant, shovel, straighten. Dig, plant, shovel, straighten. Within the allotted time, all seven trees had been planted. On their way back to the sleeping quarters, Thomas and BJ talked about how satisfying it was to actually see physical results.

"It's hard to see tangible results when one teaches yoga," Thomas explained, "except for increased flexibility, but there are intangibles."

"Such as?"

"Well, people, who have been coming to class for a while, often tell me that yoga has helped them with subtle things, like emotional control and better sleep. There have even been instances when people told me that yoga helped them through financial difficulty, a death in the family, even marital problems. I had no idea until afterward."

"That must be rewarding."

"It is."

"The only tangible changes in the investing business pertain to my bank balance," BJ explained, "and even though that is quite satisfying, I must admit that I can't wait to open a yoga studio and influence people's lives more directly."

"Until then, we'll have to settle for shoveling shit every day,"

Thomas added with a chuckle, "and see the fruits of our labor—literally. Not a bad deal."

The two men laughed.

After changing from the dirty gardening clothes into fresh ones and putting on his high-end running sneakers—the ones he was protecting from the gardening work—BJ headed for the strip mall. He was beginning to handle the heat better, seeing as he made the trek to the payphone every day. This was his fifth trip in all, the first one being on Sunday, the day after the program started. Thankfully, there were sidewalks on either side of the four-lane highway that led from the ashram to the strip mall.

Each day, BJ felt like he was entering a whole new world when he left the ashram premises. During his walks, he saw what seemed to be a never-ending stream of cars, making him wonder where everyone was going during the middle of the day, but he never saw other pedestrians. No one but him was stupid enough to go out for a walk in the middle of the day during the height of summer in Florida.

He considered himself lucky to have found a payphone. In general, payphone devices—which used to be on every street corner when he traveled to the USA in his teens—were now all but extinct. Thankfully, a gas station by the strip mall had decided that they would provide this service to their customers. Their payphone was outside, in the shade, away from the traffic.

BJ pulled out his international phone card and began the laborious process of dialing the number. First, he dialed the eight hundred number on the card, then entered his ten digit pin code, then the three digit Iceland country code, and, finally, the seven digit phone number for Sara. He got through in one try. Hearing her voice was a welcome relief.

He told her how his muscles ached, about his never ending vigilance because of all the insects, how he would shoot himself if he would hear the question, 'Is it true that Iceland is green, and Greenland is ice?' one more time, and how he was managing to stay hydrated in the heat.

Sara told him that her class attendance was going up, which was unusual for summer, about several locations she had scouted for their yoga studio, and that she had received a call from his mother, asking whether or not he was going to call because his kids were with her for the weekend.

"You should call," she said. "They really want to hear from you."

"I know," BJ replied. "I better hang up then. I only have an hour left until I have to be back at the ashram."

"Okay. Love you. We'll talk tomorrow."

"Love you too."

For the second time, BJ went through the tedious process of punching in the endless row of numbers. This time around it took two attempts. His mother answered.

"Hi, mom. It's me."

"Bjarni," she responded, in her unique chiding tone. "Why didn't you call earlier? The kids have been waiting by the phone all morning."

"Mom, there is no phone at the place where I am staying. I only have ten minutes to talk. Can you put the kids on, please?"

"I still don't understand why you are doing this silly yoga thing, Bjarni. You have a perfectly good business in Iceland. Surely, you can invest in a yoga studio without becoming a yoga teacher. I just don't understand why you would leave your children for nearly six weeks during the middle of summer, when there is no school, to learn something that you are never really going to use."

"Mom, we've talked about this before. I am not only doing this for the money. I really like yoga. I want to understand it and have the ability to deepen my own practice as I get older. Now, can you please put the kids on the phone? I don't have much time."

"Yes, yes, here they are. Your father sends his best, although he doesn't understand what you are doing there either."

"Thanks, mom," BJ replied with a sigh, "give him my regards as well."

Helgi and Hulda came on the phone and told their father all about what they had been doing since he left for Florida. The weather had been good, so they had been playing outside a lot, exploring the rocky beach near the house where their mom lived and playing in the creek next to their grandmother's house. Helgi told his dad about a new video game he was playing, and Hulda described some of the arts and crafts she had made.

"I've got to go now kids. I'll call you again this weekend," BJ said after talking to them for nearly twenty minutes. He would have to refill his phone card soon.

"We love you, dad."

"I love you too. Give each other a hug from me."

After he'd hung up the phone, BJ headed to the Subway store in the strip mall. He'd realized on the first day that he wouldn't be able to survive without lunch. Every day since he'd gotten himself a six-inch sub after his phone call with Sara. He liked Lilavati's vegetarian cooking, but he missed eating meat.

When he entered the store, the first thing he saw was a familiar face. Kurt was stuffing himself with a bloated bacon sandwich.

"Hello, mister vegan," BJ said as he sat down next to a startled Kurt. "What is that you are eating?"

"A sandwich," Kurt replied in a self-conscious tone with his mouth full.

"Yes, a bacon sandwich," BJ teased him. "I thought you didn't eat meat. In fact, I thought you didn't eat any animal products."

"Please don't tell on me," Kurt replied as he swallowed. "Bacon is my weakness. I only became a vegan because of Bea, but every time I get a chance, I eat bacon. It even goes against my religion, my culture, I am a Jew after all, but I can't help myself. I've been hiding this bacon obsession all my life."

"Your secret is safe with me," BJ said, "but I don't understand. Why lie? Why not tell people that you eat meat?"

"You want me to analyze myself?"

"Why not? You are a psychologist after all."

"Okay then," Kurt said, wiped his teeth with his tongue and put his sandwich down. "I don't tell other people that I eat bacon because I like how it feels when people think I am a vegan. Meat eaters look at me like I am somehow superior, and vegans embrace me as one of their own. I don't want to lose that."

"I understand. It's similar to when I tell people that I run marathons. It gives me instant respect. The difference is that I don't have to lie."

"Am I really lying, though? I am a vegan most of the time. I don't deserve to be punished for my weakness for bacon."

"Whatever you say," BJ said, shaking his head. "Again, your secret is safe with me."

Kurt replied with a quick thank you and then returned to devouring his sandwich. BJ grabbed one of his own, stacked with salami, ham, bacon, and pepperoni.

"You wanna walk back with me?" BJ asked after he made his purchase.

"No," Kurt replied. "No offense but people know that you leave the premises to eat meat during lunch, and I don't want to be associated with that."

"Suit yourself, but you should really rethink your strategy here. What will happen when Bea finds out that you eat meat? By then you will not only have been breaking your vegan code, but you will have been lying to her as well. This can't possibly end well for you."

"Thanks for your concern, my friend. I'll think about it," Kurt replied, swallowing the last bite of his sandwich.

"I'll see you back at the ashram."

"See you."

BJ walked in a hurry and made it back to the ashram just in time for the two o'clock class. His clothes were drenched in sweat, prompting the third change of attire that day. He would need to sign up for time in the laundry room.

Chapter Eight

"Who in here would like more energy?"

It was Friday night and Yogi Krishna Soham was lecturing. His question prompted everyone to raise their hand.

"Ahh, so you would all like more energy — but for what?" he asked. "Would you like energy to love, live, and serve more, or would you like more energy to work, struggle, and hate? Everyone wants more energy — evident by the amount of coffee and number of energy drinks sold in the world — but few ask the question why."

There was a glint in his eye when Yogi Krishna Soham paused for effect.

"I bet that most of you would like to think that you would love and serve more if you had more energy, but in reality, you would probably do more of what you are already doing."

"Why do you say that?" BJ asked without raising his hand.

"Because people are creatures of habit, my inquisitive friend from Iceland. For example, individuals who don't have much money and don't make a habit of saving or giving to charity, even in tiny amounts, will not save or give to charity when they get rich. Energy is like money. It amplifies whatever is already present. If you are a good person, more energy will amplify your goodness. If you are a bad person, more energy will make you a monster. Take the example of Hitler. He had a tremendous amount of energy — partly because he dabbled in yoga and occultism and was a self-proclaimed vegetarian — but he spent his energy on igniting World War Two and on systematically killing and oppressing the Jews."

Again, he used a dramatic pause to underline his words.

"You have to be careful when you ask for more energy," Yogi Krishna Soham added. "First, become a person who will do good. Only then should you utilize yogic techniques to increase your energy."

Most of the students were nose deep in the notebooks, writing studiously.

"In Sanskrit, energy is called prana," Yogi Krishna Soham continued. "Prana is the life force pulsing through us. It is not mystical or farfetched, but rather something that most people actively acknowledge in their everyday lives. When anyone says that another person has a lot of energy or is a low energy person, they are talking about prana. Like electricity, prana is invisible to the naked eye. We know that electricity exists because we can turn on the lights, use the washing machine or charge our electronic devices. In the same way, we know that prana exists because it is the animating force that makes our bodies move, our minds think, our tongues speak, and our emotions sizzle. Without prana, the body is a lifeless mass of deteriorating flesh."

He paused, this time to allow everyone to finish writing. It wasn't until the entire group was looking at him, eagerly waiting for more, that he continued.

"The philosophy of yoga offers a tremendous amount of information about prana, such as the philosophy of the chakras or energy wheels, the philosophy of Kundalini or serpent energy, and the philosophy of the seventy-two thousand nadis or energy channels. We will cover those ideas in the advanced three hundred hour teacher training, but tonight, I am going to introduce to you the philosophy of the gunas or energy states."

Several of the students were whispering, asking each other how to spell the Sanskrit names.

"The gunas," Yogi Krishna Soham said, raising his voice slightly, appearing irritated by the interruption, "are called tamas, rajas, and sattva. Tamas is a lethargic or degenerative state of energy, similar to a quagmire. Rajas is a dynamic and erratic state of energy, similar to a raging river in a narrow ravine. Sattva is pure and harmonious energy, similar to a calm, peaceful lake."

Chatter amongst the students continued during Yogi Krishna Soham's next pause. The yoga master waited patiently for the chatter to die down, but his enforcer and right-hand man, Govinda, could not contain himself.

"Guys! Guys!" he cried. "Have you completely forgotten the orientation? What was the first rule?"

"Not to speak while a lecture is going on," Blossom replied. She had already put down her pen and was not engaging in the chatter.

"That's right. The lectures will go very long if you always use Gurudev's pauses to whisper amongst yourselves. Please show some respect."

"It is quite alright, Govinda," Yogi Krishna Soham said in a fatherly tone. "Every group gets the exact amount of information they deserve based on the attention that they give."

The group became instantly silent. Yet, Yogi Krishna Soham did not begin speaking again. Soon the silence became deafening. No one dared to utter a word, not even the jittery aerobics teacher Poppy opened her mouth. Yogi Krishna Soham looked over the group—his expression emotionless.

"There is a lot of energy in this group," he finally said. "A lot of prana. Unfortunately, most of it is rajasik energy—plentiful, but unstable. When we meditate in the mornings, I feel it, the restlessness, the agitation, the stress, the anxiety, and the confusion. I also feel it during lectures. It has been six days now. Some of you have calmed down a little, but most of you are still at the pace of doing, doing, doing."

Several people in the group looked ashamed like they had let Yogi Krishna Soham down.

"Now, let me ask you this," he continued, without acknowledging the shameful emotions in the room. "If the purpose of yoga is to uncover that which does not change, what is the best energy state for the yogi or yogini to be in?"

The group remained silent.

"Come now," Yogi Krishna Soham prodded. "This is not a rhetorical question. What is the best energy state to be in if one wants to uncover that which does not change?"

"Sattva," the lovely Valentina replied.

"Correct, miss Valentina," Yogi Krishna Soham responded. "And why is sattva the most conducive energy state?"

"Because it is pure, calm and peaceful."

"Correct again, miss Valentina," Yogi Krishna Soham said, "which leads to my final question. Can a yogi or yogini expect to remain in the sattvik state at all times?"

"Yes, if yoga is practiced in the right way, then we yogis and yoginis should be able to remain pure and calm at all times," Valentina replied once again, sounding proud and confident.

"Unfortunately, miss Valentina, your final answer is wrong," Yogi Krishna Soham replied.

Valentina was clearly embarrassed. It was almost as if Yogi Krishna had set her up.

"Let me explain why you are wrong," he continued. "The philosophy of the gunas describes the cyclical nature of energy. Prana goes through these three states on a cyclical basis. When you wake up in the mornings, you are in a tamasik state, tired and heavy. You have to move into the rajasik state to wake up. Only when you have aroused yourself from the tamasik state and entered the rajasik state can you calm yourself down and enter the sattvik state. Furthermore, because energy moves in this cycle, if you stay in the sattvik state too long, it will turn tamasik again. Imagine staying for too long in a hot bath. Instead of feeling refreshed, you feel drained."

"I think I understand this theoretically," Andrea interjected. She'd gotten tired of sitting and was lying on her abdomen, propped up on her elbows, "but how exactly would these gunas, these energy cycles, work? And, more importantly, how does knowing about them influence our lives?"

"Those are good questions," Yogi Krishna Soham replied.

Andrea looked surprised.

"In fact, those are great questions, miss Andrea, the only questions that really matter."

She sat up as Yogi Krishna Soham continued and addressed the entire group.

"How will these ideas, these practices, influence your lives? How will they affect you, change you, improve you? Those are the questions all of you should be asking all the time. Not, will this be on the test or how is it spelled, but how will it help you uncover that which does not change?"

Yogi Krishna Soham was smiling broadly. He got excited when any of his students showed interest or displayed understanding.

"To answer your question, miss Andrea, understanding the philosophy of the gunas can greatly influence your body and mind. For example, in the tamasik state, your body will be lethargic and slow moving, and your mind will be disinterested, easily bored and unenthused."

Andrea nodded like she was intimately familiar with that state.

"To get yourself out of the tamasik state, you have to get moving. Physically, you do that by exercising the body. Mentally, you energize your mind with goals and purposeful tasks. You give your mind something to do. In English, they say that an idle mind is the devil's workshop, but in yoga, an idle mind is a tamasik mind. To wash out a quagmire, you need a raging river."

Yogi Krishna Soham expressed himself with gusto, with great energy.

"However, when the mind becomes too active and irritated, when the body becomes tense and restless, when you feel continually stressed and your attention is going in a thousand different directions, then you use breathing, relaxation and meditation techniques to transition into the sattvik energy state."

The yoga master demonstrated by taking deep breaths in rhythm with a calming hand movement.

"Yogi Krishna?" BJ asked, raising his hand. "Isn't this rajas or rajasik state, as you call it, the best energy state to be in for those of us who live and work in the Western world? It seems to be the most dynamic state, at least, it sounds like the state in which I like to work, you know, to get things done."

"Yes, mister BJ. It is true that the rajasik state can be quite useful, but if used continually it will lead to all the worst stress related symptoms imaginable. Uncontrolled rajasik energy leads to every Western lifestyle disease that yoga has been shown to cure or minimize. The key to living in the spirit of yoga is balance. You must find balance between these three energy states."

"But when we were working in the fields today," BJ replied, "planting ten banana trees in less than an hour, I can only imagine that we were using rajasik energy, right?"

"Yes and no," Govinda interjected, "if I may Gurudev."

"Go ahead," Yogi Krishna Soham replied. He used the break to release his legs from the lotus pose and shake them out to get the blood flowing again.

"To use me as an example," Govinda continued, "I can say that even though my body was in the rajasik energy, moving swiftly and with purpose, my mind was in sattvik energy, relaxed and focused singularly on the task at hand."

"Excellent illustration, Govinda," Yogi Krishna Soham complemented his disciple and assumed the lotus pose again. "There can be a tremendous difference between mind, body and emotions. Another example would be if the body were lethargic and the mind simultaneously active."

"Kind of like when I sit at the computer all day working and my mind is active, but my body is lazy?" Andrea chimed in.

"Precisely," Yogi Krishna Soham said.

"What about the balance you spoke of?" BJ asked, resting his back up against the wall, his knees bent, his notebook on his thighs.

"Well, the key is to spend as little time in tamasik energy as possible, an appropriate amount of time in rajasik energy, mainly for sustenance and physical activity, and most of the time in sattvik energy, that is, if your goal is to uncover that which does not change."

"And if that is not my goal?" Poppy blurted out.

"Then yoga is not for you. Then none of this philosophy matters," Yogi Krishna Soham answered coldly. "Lord Krishna said that out of a thousand, only one searches for the truth. The Truth, with a capital T, is the underlying essence of all things. It is that which does not change. Learning to manipulate energy is only a means to an end, used on the path towards yoga or union, it is not yoga itself. The same goes for all the other techniques. They are only a means to an end. The reason I mentioned Hitler in my introduction was to impress upon you the importance of having a worthy goal to go along with your practice. Electricity can be good or bad, depending on which device you plug into it. In the same way, prana can be good or bad, depending on the character you plug into it. I would much rather that unethical and evil people not practice yoga at all. With little energy, they can only harm themselves."

Yogi Krishna Soham stopped for a moment, took a sip of water and then stroked his beard and rearranged the mala beads around his neck before he continued.

"The purpose of yoga is to uncover that which does not change. To do that, one must dwell in the sattvik energy, which is one of harmony, compassion, purity, and peace."

"Yogi Krishna?" Valentina asked after a short pause.

"Yes, miss Valentina?"

"I am confused. You said that we cannot always be in the sattvik energy, yet you seem to be urging us to be in the sattvik energy most of the time if we want to unveil Atman."

"What is possible and what is preferable is not always the same, miss Valentina. It would be wonderful if we could dwell in the sattvik state at all times, but part of the challenge of being in this body is understanding its limitations. As human beings, we cannot help but cycle through these energies on a regular basis. Tamas is a part of life. Sometimes, we feel lethargic, drained, and sad. That is natural. Tamasik energy can even be appropriate, for example, after a loss of a loved one, when we are sick, or when we are licking our wounds, physical or emotional. Similarly, rajas is a part of life. We need energy to move, think and act, but if it goes unchecked and unbalanced, that energy can get out of control and create chaos. Trying to live in rajasik energy all the time will wreak havoc. Yes, it is the goal of the yoga practitioner to spend as much time as possible in the sattvik energy, but it is quite impossible to dwell in it at all times."

"What about holy people and saints?" Valentina pressed on. "Don't they live in the sattvik energy at all times? And if they can do it, shouldn't that be our goal as well."

"You have to discern between holy people and Avatars," Yogi Krishna Soham responded. "According to scripture, Avatars are the incarnations of God. Holy people, on the other hand, are human beings, and are, as such, subject to human limitations. They may well be able to spend more time in the sattvik state than most, but they are not immune to the energy cycle and inevitably go into tamasik and rajasik states, even if only for brief moments."

"So Jesus, for example," Valentina continued. "Was he an Avatar or a holy person?"

"That depends on how you look at it," Yogi Krishna Soham answered. "According to some scriptures, he is considered an Avatar, but others point to his emotional outbreaks, for example, when he admonished the peddlers at the temple, overthrowing their tables and screaming at them, as proof that he was merely a holy man, subject to human limitations."

"I doubt that there is such a thing as a perfect human being or holy person," BJ remarked. "Despite the stories, I've seen no evidence of it."

"That sounds very jaded," Valentina responded. "I believe in goodness and human potential. I believe that at our core we are divine and that if we work hard enough to remove obstacles, we can allow our divine energy to shine through."

"I prefer realism," BJ quickly answered. "Yes, we can all be better, but never perfect, like Yogi Krishna just said."

"Perfection! Holiness! These are only labels, only names. What matters is unveiling the Atman!" Yogi Krishna Soham stated forcefully. "A leaf on a tree should not spend all its time trying to please the other leaves. Rather, it should connect to its source, the branch, the trunk, the roots, the earth. That which does not change is our source, our essential element. It is the causal state, the atom, the quark. It is the essence from which all else comes. The sattva energy helps us unveil that state. How we appear to other human beings is secondary."

Chapter Nine

The yoga hall was lavishly decorated for a special occasion, the Sunday night Satsang or gathering of truth. Vases, filled with yellow, orange and white flowers, flanked the stage. Tea lights in glass jars had been placed all around the room. Flower wreaths hung on the walls in between the depictions of Krishna and flower petals had been strewn over the carpet. It was quite a sight. The otherwise dull and dreary hall had taken on an air of oriental mystique.

The teacher trainees had been asked to dress in white clothes if they had any. Most complied, wearing something either light beige or completely white, except BJ, who wore blue shorts and a light blue t-shirt, and Thomas, who always wore black. In addition to the teacher trainees, there were several guests in their midst, all of whom seemed to know their way around the ashram.

Govinda instructed the group to sit closer to the stage than they normally did, which meant that only half the room was filled with people. For the first time, Yogi Krishna's wife, Lilavati, was seated next to the stage, wearing a white silk sari decorated with red and green zirconia stones. She had a red mark on her forehead, and her long black hair was tied in a braid.

When the clock struck eight, Lilavati and Govinda began chanting. For accompaniment, he played the harmonium—an Indian wooden box that resembles the accordion, except that the air is pumped with one hand while the melody is played with the other —and she beat the rhythm with a tambourine. They repeated a mantra over and over again, varying the melody slightly. Soon, the group joined in. Some sang timidly with their eyes open, not sure about what was going on, while others closed their eyes, clapped their hands, sang loudly, and swayed to the hypnotizing rhythm.

Om-Namo-Bhaga-vate-Vasu-dev-ay-a, the group chanted as Yogi Krishna Soham entered the room, wearing a white silk robe and a long sandalwood mala bead necklace. His hair was slicked back, his beard combed, and his shoulders were draped with an orange ceremonial silk scarf. He walked in slowly, his eyes half-closed, chanting along with the group, stepped on the stage, sat down in one graceful movement, crossed his legs, and closed his eyes completely. He began clapping his hands in rhythm and then raised his voice, singing melodically along with the group. The music came to a crescendo with everyone singing at the top of their lungs and clapping steadily. Then, the lead singers gradually lowered their voices and slowed down until the chanting was but a whisper.

What followed was complete silence.

For the first time since the training began, everyone was calm and quiet. They sat still for ten minutes, the energy different from the morning attempts at meditation. There was no movement, no irritability, only serenity.

"Aaaauuuummmmm," Yogi Krishna Soham chanted softly to break the silence.

"Aaaauuuummmmm," the group responded.

"Aaaauuuummmmm," they chanted together several times.

Yogi Krishna Soham placed his hands in prayer pose and said: "Namaste!"

"Namaste!" the group responded in unison.

Lilavati stood up, walked to the stage, went on her knees, and bowed deeply before her husband. He held up his hands like a priest giving a blessing. Govinda followed suit, bowing deeply before his guru. The two were followed by the five guests who had joined the group for Satsang, each one putting their hands in prayer pose and bowing deeply before Yogi Krishna Soham, who responded each time by raising his hands and giving a blessing.

Blossom was the first teacher trainee to bow to Yogi Krishna Soham. Then came Valentina, Stacey, who was closely followed by Ang Lin, then Edna, Poppy, Jasmine, Gerwalta, Malin, Thomas, Betsy, and finally Camille.

BJ, Kurt, Andrea, and Laurie were the only ones who did not

bow. Thomas looked at BJ and Kurt like they had somehow betrayed him by not following suit, but they shrugged their shoulders in response.

"Jai, Jai, Sadhguru Swamidev!" Yogi Krishna Soham said, as he stood up, turned around, went on his knees, and bowed deeply before the picture of his guru.

"Jai, Jai!" Govinda, Lilavati, and several others responded, raising their hands.

"We must always pay respects to our teachers and gurus," Yogi Krishna Soham explained, after he sat down again, facing the group. "We owe them our knowledge, our wisdom. We should never disrespect those who have taught us. If we disrespect them, we disrespect our own knowledge, our own wisdom. Everything we know has been built on the foundation they provided us. We should give equal respect to our kindergarten teachers and our spiritual gurus. Both have influenced our lives in positive ways. Both deserve our respect."

Several group members bowed to Yogi Krishna Soham again.

"If water were flowing off a cliff," Yogi Krishna Soham continued, "and we were standing level to the drop off or above it, we would get no water. Only if we bowed would the water flow into our wisdom containers. Those who think they are better than the guru will not learn from the guru. Those who believe they are equal to the guru, who see him as a friend, will not learn from the guru. Only those who realize that the guru knows more than they do, those who approach him with humility, will learn from the guru. Bowing is a representation of humility. Without humility, it is a mechanical act. With humility, it signifies the student's mindset, signals that he or she is ready to learn."

Again, the yoga master's words prompted some of the people to bow, even BJ nodded slightly.

"Did you feel the quiet in the room, the sattvik energy, after the chanting?" Yogi Krishna Soham asked the group with a big grin on his face after everyone had settled down, waiting for the night's lesson.

The group responded with nods and several muted yesses.

"Chanting is a rajasik activity that leads to sattvik energy," Yogi Krishna Soham explained. "It is similar to vigorous breathing techniques or strenuous physical exercises that result in deep relaxation."

"Can we do chanting like that in the mornings, Yogi Krishna?" Poppy asked, looking out of character in her white garbs. "My mind has never quieted down like that before."

"Would you like that?" Yogi Krishna Soham queried the rest of the group. They responded with eager nods and resounding yesses.

"Good. Good," Yogi Krishna Soham said. "Tomorrow, we will begin the six o'clock meditation with chanting. Tonight, however, several guests have joined us for our traditional Sunday Satsang, and before we continue, I would like them to introduce themselves to the group. Doctorji, if you would begin," he prompted, nodding to an elderly Indian gentleman.

"Certainly, Guruji," the man responded, speaking with a thick Indian accent. He had a full head of graying hair, was noticeably thin, sported stylish black-rimmed Ralph Lauren glasses, and wore simple white pants and a collarless shirt that was lined with gold thread. "My name is Dr. Jaipur Mehta. Like Guruji, I was born in Porbandar, which is in the Gujarat province. I have lived in the USA for almost thirty-five years now, practicing medicine since I was twenty-eight. Unfortunately, I was not introduced to yoga until I was forty-five. It changed my life. I own a house in a nearby neighborhood and come here to learn from Guruji and to be in his auspicious energy every time I get the chance."

Yogi Krishna Soham bowed to the doctor and then nodded to the next of the five guests.

"Hi everyone," a thin and athletic woman in her mid-twenties said. "My name is Lulu. I am a massage therapist. I come here two to three times a week with my massage table. If any of you are feeling sore and want me to help you feel better, let me know."

"Yes, please!" Andrea blurted out. "I desperately need some of that."

"I'll probably book a standing reservation too," BJ said with a smile.

"Count me in," the sixty-two-year-old Betsy Brigham said.

"Okay then," a delighted Lulu replied. "Talk to me after the Satsang. I come here as often as I can for classes. Yogi Krishna is an awesome teacher, Lilavati a fantastic cook, and Govinda is a good friend," she added, giving Govinda the nod, making him blush a little. "I look forward to getting to know all of you."

Yogi Krishna Soham thanked her and then pointed to the next guest.

"Sincere greetings to all of you, distinguished group of yoga teacher trainees," a heavyset woman in her late fifties said as she stood up. She brushed her gray stricken black hair away from her face and continued with her ceremonial introduction. "My birth name was Patricia Erhardt, but you may call me Rukmini, which was the name of the first wife of Krishna, a truly auspicious name given to me by Gurudev."

She cleared her throat before she continued in a haughty tone.

"You are all very lucky to be here learning from this great man. Gurudev saved my life ten years ago. I was depressed, lonely and suffering from a deep attachment to Maya — which is the Sanskrit name for our ever changing dualistic world of light and shadows. Gurudev took me under his wing, taught me yoga, and helped me to uncover my soul. I know that I still have a long way to go, but thanks to the grace of Gurudev, I am in safe hands. He guides me every step of the way."

She then turned to the stage, fell on her knees, and shouted: "Jai, Jai, Sadhguru Yogi Krishna Soham!"

"Namaste, Rukmini," the yoga master replied.

"Namaste, Gurudev," she said and sat back down, wearing a tearful smile, looking at Yogi Krishna Soham like he was the Lord himself.

"Next, I want to introduce you to one of my most devoted students," Yogi Krishna Soham stated. "She took my yoga teacher training two years ago and has come in for weekly private classes ever since. I gave her the name Sunita, the one with good morals. You would all do well to model her dedication."

"Thank you, Yogiji," a small woman in her early thirties with shoulder-length curly hair, delicate facial features, brown eyes, and an unusually large nose, which strangely enough did not detract from her beauty, replied. Like the other guests, she was wearing all white. She did not stand up and spoke in a low voice.

"I don't know quite what to say. I am Alyssa Floros or Sunita like Yogiji said. He is a never ending well of wisdom. The private classes with him provide me with inspiration to teach my yoga classes and live by a higher ethical standard. It's nice to meet all of you."

Sunita's introduction got a positive response from the group.

"Good to meet you as well, Sunita," Valentina said.

"Yes, good to meet you," others echoed.

Yogi Krishna Soham smiled approvingly, then nodded towards the one guest who still hadn't introduced herself.

"Hi, everyone. My name is Tiffany Rotrosen, and I am a forty-four-year-old stay at home mom and freelance journalist. I help Yogi Krishna with his books and in return, I get to come to his yoga classes and Satsang."

"I couldn't write a single word without Sucheta," Yogi Krishna Soham interrupted.

"Oh yes, I forgot to tell you that," the shorthaired, wide-eyed, brunette replied. "Yogi Krishna gave me the name Sucheta, which means one with a beautiful mind. You can call me that or Tiffany. I don't mind. You'll probably see me around a lot. I come to classes several times a week and spend about ten hours a week on writing projects with Yogi Krishna."

"Yes," Yogi Krishna Soham interrupted again. "We are working on a major writing project now, titled *The Spiritual Heritage of Yoga: Understanding the Gita and the Sutras*. We will talk more about it in the advanced teacher training."

"Yeah, that project is coming along nicely," Tiffany replied, "and… that's about it. Nice to meet all of you."

"You too," the group echoed.

"Namaste, Sucheta," Yogi Krishna Soham said.

"Namaste, Yogi," she replied.

"Now that the introductions are done, we will proceed with our traditional Indian Satsang," Yogi Krishna Soham stated. "You see, in India, the guru does not prepare for lectures like we do here in the West. No. In India, the guru only responds to questions. If there are no questions, the guru is silent. Thusly, the Satsang becomes an interplay between the guru and the group." The yoga master straightened his back, opened his arms like he was embracing the students, and said: "Ask away."

Chapter Ten

"The two of you sold me out tonight," Thomas said with an uneasy grin when the three roommates were back in their sleeping quarters after the Satsang. As usually, Ang Lin was nowhere to be seen. He only spent a few hours in their room each night. Kurt and BJ had gotten comfy in their bottom bunks, while Thomas sat on the floor instead of climbing into his top bunk.

"What do you mean?" BJ replied.

"When I bowed at the feet of Yogi Krishna Soham, neither one of you followed. Why?"

"The better question is, why did you decide to bow?" Kurt responded.

"I don't know," Thomas answered honestly. "I guess it was just a when-in-Rome situation. Everyone was doing it, so I followed suit. It seemed like the right thing to do."

"Classic herd mentality," Kurt replied. "I prefer to stand on my own two feet, Thomas. Maybe Yogi Krishna Soham is worth bowing to, but if and when I decide to bow, it will be on my own terms."

"Hey, don't say that," Thomas responded, sounding offended. "I pride myself on standing on my own two feet. I just thought that it couldn't hurt. Bowing is simply a gesture of respect."

"I've never bowed to anyone in my life," BJ said. "Just nodding a little after he spoke to us about respecting our teachers was hard for me. Authority resistance is in the DNA of us Vikings, you know."

"Yeah, well," Thomas replied, "I'm sorry you guys feel that way. I'm happy I bowed. I respect him as a teacher."

Chirping crickets became audible as the three men fell silent for a few moments, thinking about everything that had transpired that night. Yogi Krishna Soham had taken questions for over an hour about everything from poses to philosophy to the guru-disciple relationship.

"Aside from the bowing, I really liked what Yogi Krishna had to say tonight," BJ finally said. "I especially liked how he spoke about philosophy like a pair of tinted glasses, how there are two ways of painting the world purple, either with brush and bucket—an infuriating and impossible task—or by putting on purple glasses. I've never really thought about philosophy in that way before."

"I agree," Thomas said, shifting on the floor. "I liked how he took Stacey's question—'Why do we need all this philosophy when we will mostly be teaching yoga postures?'—and turned it upside down, explained how everyone had their own personal philosophy of life, how everything that we have been taught and everything that we have experienced influences how we perceive the world and how that guides our behavior. According to him, we all have a philosophy that guides us. The question is just whether or not the philosophy is any good."

"Yeah, that answer seemed to shut her up," BJ said and laughed.

"From a psychological standpoint, there is some truth to the idea that changing the color of your glasses can change your perspective, even though it is somewhat simplistic," Kurt chimed in. "Despite the fact that most everyone wants to believe that they can change everything about themselves, certain characteristics seem to be built into our DNA. We can choose our philosophy, our tinted glasses, but only to a degree."

Kurt sat on his bottom bunk and faced the two men as he spoke.

"I must say, though, that my favorite part of the Q&A session was when he talked about the stain on a white piece of cloth. I think that is the best metaphor for character improvement I have ever come across."

"That's saying something, coming from a psychologist," Thomas replied, unwrapping a Power Bar.

"Well," Kurt continued, "the metaphor perfectly describes other people's reactions when a person is trying to change. Let's take, for example, an alcoholic who has really messed up his life. That's the equivalent of a dirty shirt. What happens when he begins to clean up his act, you know, wake up at a reasonable hour, show up for work, spend time with his kids?"

"That's easy. He get's praised," BJ said, now also sitting up. "I am all too familiar with this. I have worked with several recovering alcoholics over the years, and it always pissed me off when they got praised for things that regular people did without thinking about them."

"There is a reason to praise them," Kurt explained, "because, in comparison with what the recovering alcoholic was used to doing, these behaviors, which we consider normal, are in fact abnormal for them. Their positive actions or white spots become extremely visible on a dirty background. That's why people notice. It's all about context."

"I guess," BJ grunted.

"According to this same metaphor," Kurt continued, apparently excited about the concept, "people, who are trying to do good and be good, suffer from the opposite effects. Their remaining stains become painfully obvious. For example, we see things in the behavior of Yogi Krishna Soham and Govinda that we would probably overlook if they weren't trying to be good. If Joe in the mailroom or Anna the executive would display the same behaviors, which we consider stainful — for a lack of a better word — in relation to our yoga master and his disciple, we would think nothing of them. At the most, we would say that they were in a bad mood or something. But we wouldn't judge Anna and Joe. Why? Because we don't expect that much from them, right? It's all about context."

"So, you're saying that the lower our expectations are," BJ mirrored, "the more we notice the few good deeds that those people engage in and, conversely, the higher our expectations are, the more sensitive we become to the few but visible character flaws?"

"Exactly," Kurt said enthusiastically. "We judge people, such as priests and spiritual teachers, with a different measuring stick than we judge others. Why? Because we expect more from them. The same goes for personal trainers and nutrition therapists. We can eat chocolate, but they can't."

"I don't know," Thomas said in visible frustration, crumpling up his Power Bar wrapper. "Doesn't this concept simply give an easy way out? I understand that there can be some faults, that people are human, but shouldn't people, who put themselves in a position to teach others, practice what they preach? Aren't we justifiably outraged by hypocrites?"

"Yeah, what about that?" BJ agreed. "Shouldn't we expect something from people like that? I agree with Thomas. It sounds like an easy way out, a way to deflect from flaws, to refrain from dealing with them."

"Sure, that's one way to look at it," Kurt replied, "but then you are demanding perfection. Do you believe that there is such a thing?"

"Not based on what I've seen and experienced," BJ answered.

"That has been my perception as well. Perfection seems to be an ideal, not a reality," Kurt said, "but I understand your frustration, Thomas. You ask if people who teach others shouldn't at least do most of what they teach? My answer to that would be, yes, of course they should. I am not talking about complete hypocrites, people who do the opposite in private of what they preach in public. I am, however, acknowledging that people are people. We are all human, and when we try to stick a label of perfection on another person, we will invariably be disappointed. Only dead people get labels of perfection and holiness because we can no longer see their faults. In fact, we can imagine whatever we want about them."

"Didn't Yogi Krishna allude to that tonight?" BJ pondered. "He said something about the guru being like a fire, too close and you get burned, too far away and you get no heat."

"Yes, because when we get too close," Kurt replied, "we cannot help but see the stains."

"So, where does that leave us?" Thomas asked earnestly and threw the wrapper in the trash.

"I guess it means that we should learn what we can from our yoga master and leave the rest," BJ said, trying to sound like the elder in the room, which he was in terms of years, although, more often than not, he didn't feel like it. "I think figuring out this stain on a white piece of cloth thing is a lot like performing a SWOT analysis before making an investment," he continued. "You look at the strengths and opportunities, but you also acknowledge the weaknesses and threats. The threat in a learning situation like this is placing the teacher on a pedestal, imitating both his admirable qualities and less desirable faults. The metaphor reminds us to stay on our toes and not take anything at face value. My biggest problem with Yogi Krishna," BJ said in response to his own contemplation, "is that he seems to be saying all the right things when it comes to the teacher-student relationship, but at the same time he appears to revel in his role as supreme authority. He seems to insist that he is always right, and he has his students, even his wife, bow to him. To me, those behaviors are stains. I see a lot of good in him and what he teaches, but I feel like it's going to take a lot of work for me to continually discern between what I can learn from him and what I should dismiss."

"It could be that," Thomas interjected, "but you could also be experiencing a clash of cultures. I told you guys before that the Indian way of teaching tends to be authoritarian and patriarchal. His behavior may represent a stain when compared with our pluralistic and feminist worldviews, but in India, his approach to teaching is totally acceptable."

"Even if I were to accept that, discerning between what is a stain and what is a white piece of cloth sounds like an awful lot of work," BJ replied.

"The beauty is that Yogi Krishna gave us a perfect philosophical tool to use for that purpose," Kurt said, maintaining his excitement. "Without his stain on a white piece of cloth metaphor, we wouldn't even be talking about this. We would be lost in utter frustration. That's why I like the idea. It gives us a reference point."

"True," BJ responded.

"I guess," Thomas added.

"I remember reading a popular psychology book when I was in

college," Kurt said with a look of contemplation on his face, "a book that was not respected in academic circles. I read it under the covers. To my surprise, I genuinely liked many of the ideas that the author was putting forth and began using them liberally in my studies. Then, about halfway through the book, the author began to speak about his sincere belief in Jesus Christ. I was appalled. Not only did I believe that religion had no place in psychology, but I also believed that being religious was tantamount to a psychological disorder. I threw the book away and stopped using his ideas, even the ones that had sounded reasonable to me until that point."

Kurt paused for effect before he continued his story.

"Then, years later, I decided to read the book again. Aside from a few religious references — the ones that had caused me to throw the book out earlier — the book was fantastic. I still use many of his ideas in my work today."

"Are you saying that the stain concept is similar to not throwing the baby out with the bathwater?" Thomas inquired.

"Similar, yes," Kurt replied, raising his eyebrows, "but the two refer to different aspects. Not throwing the baby out with the bathwater reminds us that there is a kernel of truth in most everything and that we shouldn't throw out the essential with the inessential. The stain idea reminds us not to overreact to faults in people we admire and want to learn from. Both concepts encourage us to refrain from black or white thinking."

"Which means that we will be having several more of these conversations," BJ said in exasperation, "in the coming weeks, about what is a stain and what isn't."

"That shouldn't make you sad," Kurt replied. "I am getting as much out of these conversations as I am from the program itself."

"I agree," Thomas said. "Even though I may have been less than thrilled when you guys began criticizing Yogi Krishna and Govinda on our first night here, I have to admit that our conversations have helped me to put the ideas we are learning about into perspective."

"Sure, but, at the same time, these conversations weren't exactly what I thought I'd be doing here," BJ said, shaking his head, "which reminds me," he continued, "we are supposed to start teaching later this week. I know you are ready to teach Thomas—being a yoga teacher and all—but what about you Kurt?"

"I think so," Kurt replied, "I mean, teaching yoga poses isn't exactly rocket science."

"No, it's not rocket science, but let me tell you from experience," Thomas explained as he got up off the floor, "that in the beginning, it can be tremendously difficult to create a clear connection between words and actions. People, in general, are used to expressing their thoughts and emotions, but very few people describe what they do physically. My teacher, Yogi Vasudev, told me to start narrating my movements to create a neural link between words and actions, you know, by saying, I am raising my right hand, lowering my right hand, taking a step forward with my left foot, rolling from the heel to the toes, and so forth. It sounds ridiculous, but it worked."

"I am opening my mouth and moving my lips to talk," Kurt said like a robot and laughed.

"What about the Sanskrit words for poses?" BJ asked, ignoring Kurt's attempt at humor. "Do we have to learn them?"

"Yogi Krishna Soham hasn't said anything about whether or not to teach in Sanskrit," Kurt remarked, "nor has Govinda."

"Yogi Vasudev said that teaching in Sanskrit was for flavor, not for substance," Thomas explained. "He said that it was like going to an Italian restaurant where the menu items were in Italian. It may look good, but the waiter will have to explain everything if you don't speak Italian. I have taught in English ever since I started teaching yoga and not once has a person asked me for the Sanskrit name of a pose."

"That sounds reasonable enough, but I will be teaching in Icelandic. For this program, though, I still need to know if we are supposed to learn the Sanskrit names or not," BJ said, sounding a little frustrated.

"I don't know," Thomas replied, climbing into his top bunk. "All

I know is that Sanskrit words don't help students. If you say the Sanskrit name of a pose, then you have to follow up by telling people what the word means. I tried it for a while, but with new students being added all the time, I gave up. English works for me. If anything, I would rather learn how to teach in Spanish than in Sanskrit. That is my practical take on the matter."

"Well said," Kurt responded. "I like your reasoning."

"Shit," BJ blurted out when he looked at his watch. "It's almost midnight. We should really get to bed."

"Yes, guys," Kurt said, doing his best impression of Govinda's accent, even though it made him sound more like Arnold Schwarzenegger than Yogi Krishna's right-hand man. "Lights out."

Ang Lin opened the door cautiously.

"It's okay, Ang Lin," BJ said. "We're not asleep yet."

"Hi," Ang Lin replied. "Sorry for coming in so late."

"That wife of yours really keeps you busy," Kurt said, still using his Schwarzenegger impression.

Ang Lin grinned and made his way into the top bunk without replying.

"Leave the poor guy alone," BJ said with a smirk. "He's worn out."

"Good night," Thomas said somberly, refusing to partake in the heckling, even if it was on friendly terms.

"Good night," the other three replied with varying degrees of audibility.

BJ reached for the switch and turned off the lights. Within minutes, all of them were sleeping.

Chapter Eleven

"Ugh! I hate cleaning," Andrea said while scrubbing the stainless steel kitchen in the dining hall. It was Monday, the day after the first Satsang. Because it was raining outside, the hour of service took place inside. BJ and Andrea had been assigned the job of cleaning the kitchen.

"I have a maid that cleans my apartment every two weeks, and I only use my cleaning supplies when I absolutely have to," she complained, "I came here to learn yoga — not clean somebody's kitchen."

"Come now," BJ replied. He was on his knees scrubbing the oven, which was supposed to be self-cleaning, but Yogi Krishna and Lilavati didn't like to use that feature so they always had it cleaned by hand — at least, that's what they said. "This seva or service hour is part of the program. I can't say I like it either, but let's just get it over with."

"Yeah, yeah," Andrea replied, pouting.

"We can sing or chat to pass the time," BJ said, trying to sound optimistic.

"You clearly haven't heard me sing," Andrea said with a frustrated chuckle.

"Talking it is then," BJ responded with a smile. "What did you girls talk about after the Satsang last night?"

"The guests of course. What else? That Patricia or Rukmini or whatever her name was is some piece of work, huh?"

"Yes, she is quite the character."

"Soooo ceremonial. She treated Yogi Krishna like he was a holy man. She must have been in one heck of a bind when she came to him several years ago if she treats him this way today. I mean, the level of reverence was over the top."

"It was — wasn't it? All the bowing and stuff. I noticed that you didn't participate in that either."

"I am not the bowing kind, my friend. I told you — I'm bossy," Andrea said with zest, sporting a witty smile.

"Me, Viking," BJ said, deepening his voice. "Me not bow."

The two giggled as they kept cleaning.

"Are we being too arrogant, though?" BJ added a moment later. "I mean, what's the harm in bowing?"

"There probably isn't any harm — except to my ego — but bowing just isn't for me. I have never had an easy time deferring to authority. It just rubs me the wrong way."

"Same here," BJ replied, "I just asked to see how you'd respond."

"Why you sneaky..." Andrea said, shaking her fist at BJ.

They both laughed. She moved her bucket and sponge over to the table and began cleaning the table surface. BJ was still scrubbing the sides of the oven.

"This oven is filthy," he said. "Almost as filthy as my oven after I roast a leg of lamb. I don't get it. There is never any meat in here. They must use cooking oil or something else that splatters."

"Whatever," Andrea replied. "I confess. I've never cleaned an oven."

"Never cleaned an oven?" BJ responded skeptically. "Then your oven must either be covered in muck, or you never cook."

"You got me. I don't cook."

"Not at all?"

"Nope. I've always been on my own. Never saw the need to learn how. It's less expensive and easier to buy prepared meals or takeout."

"That's not very healthy."

"Don't you think I am aware of that genius? I am not exactly hiding the fact that I am fat."

"Why do you do that?"

"What?"

"Become argumentative and defensive when someone mentions healthy food or your physical appearance. I noticed that you did the same thing when Laurie tried to compliment you the other day."

"What are you — a shrink?"

"No, but I am bunking with one, so I guess it's rubbing off on me."

"Well, I am in no mood to be psychoanalyzed."

"Suit yourself."

They kept cleaning in silence. BJ finished the oven and turned his attention to mopping the floor. Andrea started wiping the dining room tables, hunched over because they were so low to the floor.

"Ugh! This is even less fun when we don't talk," Andrea finally blurted out. "What did you guys talk about after last night's Satsang?"

"Mostly ideas, you know."

"You're useless. When will I get any good gossip from you? At least I found out that Tiffany — or Sucheta, as Yogi Krishna likes to call her — spends an awful lot of time alone with the yoga master."

"Isn't that normal?" BJ replied. "I mean, she is helping him write his books. You're not suggesting that they are having an affair."

"I don't know," Andrea responded, "but it wouldn't surprise me. Stranger things have happened."

"I am not ready to entertain that idea," BJ said. "Yogi Krishna is an old and devout man. He doesn't seem to be interested in sex — not even a little bit. Plus, I think that Tiffany is the most interesting of all the guests that came here yesterday. I have been reading Yogi Krishna's books and based on the way he talks, I guess that Tiffany does more writing than he does."

"See. You can be good at gossiping as well if you just put your mind to it."

"I am not gossiping, just speculating."

"Potato — potato," Andrea replied. "Don't be so sensitive. Everyone does it. It's human nature to want to know about other people and 'speculate' about their motives. To your point, though, I agree. I think that Tiffany was the most interesting of the bunch, except maybe for Lulu. I can't wait to get a massage. My lower back is killing me."

"I agree, I am looking forward to getting a massage as well."

"Lulu and Tiffany were at least more interesting than the 'auspicious' Dr. India and miss little-greek-goddess-goody-two-shoes-teacher's-pet."

"There you go again. Why do you sneer at people who seem to be genuinely nice? You did the same with Valentina, although you have nothing on her."

"Look BJ," Andrea said, taking a break from her cleaning duties to look directly at him. "I am fifty-two. I have been around the block a time or two. So have you. We shouldn't have to beat around the bush. In my experience, anyone who portrays themselves as completely pure or holy is hiding something. So, yes, when I see people like Valentina and little Sunita, a little vomit gushes into the back of my mouth, because I know that the image they are trying to project can't possibly be real. That's why I sneer. And for the record, I haven't been wrong yet."

"What happened to the American motto of innocent until proven guilty?"

"That's only in the movies my Icelandic friend. Only in the movies."

"Well, I don't agree with that view, at least not yet. Maybe I will when I am in my fifties. I still want to give people the benefit of the doubt."

"Suit yourself."

"Tell me," BJ said as both of them returned to work, putting the finishing touches on their cleaning project. "Is there anything you do like about this teacher training?"

"You've judged me all wrong, BJ. I love this teacher training. I am getting so much out of it, both physically and mentally. Yes, my body is sore, and yes, I may judge people a little harshly, but this is the best time I've had in a long time."

"That's good to hear," BJ replied with a smile. "I actually like the training as well, especially the physical part. The yoga exercises are beginning to loosen up years of tightness from running."

"That must be the balancing effect that Yogi Krishna keeps talking about. You are loosening up the stiffness while I am firming up the putty. Who knows? Maybe we'll meet halfway?"

The two of them walked around the room to see if they had missed anything.

"Will you look at that," Andrea finally said. "We're done, and it's not even twelve o'clock."

It was true. The room was spotless.

"Yep. Looks clean. I'm going to head over to the barn. You coming?"

"I'll stay here for a while," Andrea replied. "I am going to use the break to practice my teaching in the yoga hall. Even if I am a teacher, I have never taught exercises in my life."

"Okay. See you at two."

"See ya."

BJ slid on his flip-flops and ran between buildings using the foliage over the walkway to shield himself from the rain. When he entered the seating area, the group of women seated there went completely silent.

"It's okay girls. It's just our friend BJ — the guy from Iceland," Laurie said to the other women who were huddled together in the corner. They breathed a collective sigh of relief.

"What were you talking about," BJ asked, "and who are you hiding it from?"

"We didn't want Govinda to overhear us," Stacey responded in her masculine voice. If she had a volume button in her toolbox, she never used it.

"Yes," Valentina chimed in, sounding all the more pleasing in contrast with Stacey. "We were just talking about how conservative this yoga teacher training is."

Poppy and Jasmine nodded in agreement.

"How so?" BJ inquired and took a seat.

"Govinda and Yogi Krishna don't like how we dress," Poppy explained.

"What?" BJ replied disbelievingly.

"It is true," Jasmine said in her thick Latino accent. "Govinda asked me not to show my belly button. I am a belly dancer. I only have clothes that show my belly button!"

"He's talked to all of us," Valentina added. "Told us to cover our cleavage — to dress in moderation."

"Yeah, we're expecting him to bring out the headscarves any day now," Laurie said defiantly.

"Has he explained why?" BJ asked, still confused.

"He has told us that it is in the 'spirit of yoga' to dress modestly, so as not to stir up any feelings of arousal during yoga class," Stacey replied. "That's how male domination always begins, you know, men fearing female sexuality, not being able to keep it in their pants."

"Isn't that taking the argument a little too far?" BJ replied. "I understand that you are upset, but if you generalize and use the argument that men can't keep it in their pants, you've lost in my opinion."

"I don't see how," Stacey replied. "Men are pigs who only have one thing on their mind. If they can't stand a little cleavage, they should stay out of the yoga class."

"That's a very standoffish attitude, Stacey," BJ said, gearing up for a fight. "Govinda is not telling you to stop being women, rather he is advocating moderation —"

"More than that," Poppy interjected. "He's telling me that I can't wear the activewear that I use during my aerobics classes. Sure, I get some advances from men, but nothing that I can't handle. People at the gym are not complaining that I dress too skimpily."

"Yeah," Laurie chimed in. "The female body is a beautiful thing. Why cover it up?"

"Hey, calm down," BJ responded. "I am on your side. If it were my class, you could wear anything you wanted to wear. I just disagreed with the argument that men can't keep it in their pants. By saying that, you are saying that sexuality is only on the male side of the equation, that women play no role in enticing and arousing men, that there is no interplay between the sexes. You are laying the blame for what happens between two adults squarely on the male side. What does that say about women, that they are always victims?"

"No, I am saying that women don't have sex on their minds all the time, not like men do," Stacey replied, holding up her end of the argument.

"Okay," BJ replied, trying to find common ground. "Let's say that men are more sexual than women, just for arguments sake, although I could probably find statistics, or at the very least opinions, to the contrary—"

"I could back you up on that," Laurie interrupted.

"Even if that were true," BJ continued, sticking to his guns, "a vast majority of men can still 'keep it in their pants' if women do not agree to have sex with them. Only in the case of rape, which is a despicable act of violence and dominance, would my argument be invalid. What I am saying is that it always takes two people to engage in consensual sex. So, when you lay the blame only on men, you are effectively saying that women play no role."

"I understand what you are saying," Stacey said, "but I don't agree with it at all. If women are being asked to cover up, it is because men are afraid that they can't keep it in their pants."

"Then we'll have to agree to disagree on that particular point. I must ask, though—not that I am trying to make Govinda and Yogi Krishna Soham right and you wrong—could there be any other practical or sensible reason why people should dress modestly in yoga class, both men and women?"

"No," Stacey retorted. "It's all about control."

"Come now," BJ said, "at least think about it before you answer. Couldn't there be any other logical reason for wanting yoga students to dress modestly?"

Stacey crossed her arms in defiance, but Valentina, Jasmine, Poppy and Laurie seemed to be thinking about it.

"I guess there could be at least one reason," Valentina finally answered.

"Yes?" BJ responded.

"In some of the spiritual books I have read over the years, it says that sexuality has been wrongfully demonized by the church over the years and that instead of seeing it that way, sex should be regarded as a beautiful and natural thing." She paused. "However, some of the books also note that sexuality can be a disturbing force. When humans are fully engaged in unbridled eroticism, they can think of nothing else. Such intense arousal can become an obstacle to those who want to be spiritual."

"But most people aren't going to yoga class for spirituality," Laurie interrupted. "They just do yoga for the exercise, so being slightly aroused might actually be good for them."

"Then I guess it depends on the type of yoga class one is attending how one should dress," Valentina responded thoughtfully, evidently struggling with the idea. "If it were purely a physical yoga class, then dress code wouldn't matter, but if the intent was to be more introverted and to avoid distractions—to be more spiritual— then I guess dressing modestly could make sense."

"Could that be where Govinda and Yogi Krishna Soham are coming from?" BJ asked cautiously. "I don't know, but—and I can't believe that I am defending them—maybe you should refrain from jumping to conclusions and think that they are somehow trying to dominate you because they ask you to dress more modestly."

"Baggy clothes are so uncomfortable when I exercise," Poppy said, "and I don't have any other clothes. They'll just have to deal with the fact that this is how I dress."

"Me too," Laurie agreed.

"Me three," the rest of the women said in unison.

"Look BJ, I know you are trying to be reasonable," Stacey said, "and if it were only the clothing, I wouldn't react quite so viscerally, but it's also the bowing. I mean, who in this day and age has their wife, their partner, bow to them like an emperor's subject? Yes, I bowed too, but only because everyone else was doing it. Overall, I think that Yogi Krishna and Govinda are too conservative, too patriarchal in their approach. I'm not going to make a big deal out of it because I am leaving next weekend, but those of you who are staying for the five weeks might want to broach the subject."

Valentina, Laurie, and Poppy looked at each other.

"We'll have to think about it," Valentina finally said. The other two nodded. "Maybe they have a better reason than we give them credit for."

"Well, I for one will not be dominated by men telling me how to dress," Laurie said fiercely while shaking her fist, although everyone could see she had a glint in her eye, that she was willfully overdoing it. "I will not flaunt my boobs, but I will wear what I brought with me. So will the other girls."

"Okay then. You have my full support," BJ said, trying to sound fatherly.

"Do you think you'll be able to keep it in your pants?" Laurie asked jokingly.

The women exploded into laughter.

"I'll see you later ladies," BJ said, shaking his head and dismissing their laughter while walking towards his room with half a smile.

Chapter Twelve

"Tomorrow you will begin teaching," Yogi Krishna Soham stated. "Are there any question about that before we start tonight's lecture?"

It was Wednesday night, and the group was gathered in the yoga hall. It was the first time since the program began, eleven days prior, that BJ felt comfortable sitting on the floor. It wasn't only because his body was becoming more malleable, but also because he had done very little sitting throughout the day.

He'd begun his day in the kitchen with Lilavati. Each morning, one person from the group would help her prepare breakfast. It had been his turn. Instead of sitting for an hour and then practicing yoga postures for another hour, as had become his daily ritual, BJ had worked at a slow but steady pace alongside Yogi Krishna Soham's wife while preparing breakfast. Lilavati had been calm to the point of being docile. She had given directions every now and then, humming with her devotional music in between, but, even though she didn't speak much, BJ had found Lilavati a joy to be around. She had a comforting presence, and her cooking skills were exquisite. Dressed in a green and yellow sari, the heavyset woman flowed from one task to another with graceful movements. BJ had sincerely enjoyed their time together, opposite to what he'd expected.

After breakfast, the group had spent most of their day with Govinda and Yogi Krishna Soham refining poses and going over teaching techniques, getting everyone ready for the days ahead. None of the girls had protested the dress code. Most had even dressed more modestly than they were used to.

Lulu, the massage therapist, had arrived in the afternoon, and BJ, Andrea, and Betsy had gotten their much-needed massages. Lulu was an expert at her craft and robust enough to break through BJ's stiff muscle tissue, especially in his lower back, shoulders, and thighs. The experience had been thoroughly professional on all levels.

All this — combined with the increased flexibility from practicing yoga every day — allowed BJ to sit cross-legged in the middle of the floor with only two pillows for support, unlike his usual position, sitting up against the wall with three to four pillows and a couple of blankets.

"Four of you will teach tomorrow," Yogi Krishna Soham said, when no hands were raised in response to his prompt for questions, "then six on Friday and six on Saturday. Also, remember that the written test is on Saturday night. If all goes well, then you will graduate this Sunday."

He looked over the room with an expression of accomplishment on his face. For a while, he didn't say anything. The students in the room were excited about the fact that they would be teaching over the next three days. However, unlike what had happened earlier in the program — when the teacher's silence prompted nervous movement and chatter — the group sat still and most of the students met the yoga master's gaze in a relaxed way.

"Tonight," Yogi Krishna Soham finally said, "I am going to talk about the ethical foundation of yoga — the yamas and niyamas."

Notebooks came out. Pens and pencils were brandished. Aside from the first lecture — when the yoga master had told the students not to write — writing vigorously was now the group's modus operandi, at least while Yogi Krishna Soham spoke.

"Some say that the yamas and niyamas are like the Ten Commandments of yoga," Yogi Krishna Soham continued. "Those who say that don't really understand yoga at all. Yoga is not about creating a peaceful and ethical society. Yoga is not a religion. Yoga is not law. Yoga is a personal path meant to unveil what?"

"That which does not change," the group responded.

The concept had been repeated at every turn during the program.

"Exactly. That which does not change," Yogi Krishna Soham responded. "The ethical guidelines, known as the yamas and niyamas, may result in ethical behavior towards other human beings, but their primary purpose is to remove internal obstacles so that the yogi or yogini can unveil Atman."

Yogi Krishna turned to his right and called: "Govinda!"

"Yes, Gurudev," the young man sprang to attention.

"Please bring out the whiteboard that I wrote on earlier today."

"As you wish, Gurudev."

Govinda bowed deeply and then hurried into the hallway. He quickly returned with a whiteboard and put it up next to the stage.

"As you can see," Yogi Krishna Soham continued, "there are five yamas and five niyamas. For the purpose of this two hundred hour program, we will cover them briefly, but those of you who are in the five hundred hour program can expect more discussion. Let us begin with the five yamas. They refer to self-control, suppressing animal instincts that we all have."

Several of the students looked up from their notebooks, visually disgusted by the thought of being compared to animals.

"Oh, you don't think you have animal instincts, do you?" Yoga Krishna Soham responded without anyone raising the question. "You are wrong. We all have animal instincts. A fetus goes through a progression of several animal states while becoming a human being, which means that sexual aggression, a sense of preservation, and seeds of violence, are all etched in our DNA. If a person is to achieve the state of yoga, of union with that which does not change, then these animal instincts must be overcome. We are animals that are capable of divinity, but we have to work for it."

He pointed at the whiteboard.

"The first yama or refraining principle is ahimsa or nonviolence. Those who want to unveil that which does not change need to abstain from violence in thought, word, and deed. That means not physically abusing another person or animal — which is why yogis and yoginis are vegetarians — and not speaking ill of others."

BJ raised his hand.

"Yes, BJ?"

"Didn't you say that Hitler was a vegetarian?"

"Yes, I did," Yogi Krishna Soham answered with a sigh, "but nonviolence is more than not eating meat. Nonviolence is the guiding light for the yoga practitioner, not a mechanical discipline. The same goes for all these guidelines."

"So, would you say that there could be instances where vegetarians display more violence than meat eaters?" Laurie asked, joining the conversation.

"That could happen," Yogi Krishna Soham answered. "However, let me caution you not to use other people's failings to justify your own. Remember, the yamas and niyamas are not about creating a perfect society, but rather about finding internal harmony so that one may uncover—"

"—that which does not change," the students sounded out again, right on cue.

"Exactly. Moving on," Yogi Krishna Soham said, rearranging his legs. "The second yama or refraining principle is satya or truthfulness. In the traditional sense, satya is about not lying, but it also refers to exaggeration and gossip as forms of untruthfulness."

At the mention of gossip, BJ looked over at Andrea with a mischievous smile on his face. In return, she imitated a silent growl and stuck her tongue out at him.

"A person that is truthful creates harmony between thoughts, words, and deeds," Yogi Krishna Soham continued, oblivious to the exchange. "Most of your internal demons are awakened when you think one thing, say another, and then do the third. Internal inconsistency is bound to create problems. Conversely, when all three are in harmony, a person cannot help but be happy."

Yogi Krishna Soham allowed his words to sink in.

"According to yoga philosophy, truth should be satyam, true, shivam, good for all, and sundaram, promote beauty and happiness."

"That is beautiful," Valentina responded, her nose deep in her notebook. "Could you repeat that please, Yogi Krishna?"

"Certainly, miss Valentina," he responded. In spite of their first interaction, on the day that the program began, Valentina had become one of his favorite students. "Satyam, true. Shivam, good for all. Sundaram, promote beauty and happiness."

"Does that mean that there are times when it's okay to lie," Kurt said.

"Why would you say that?" Valentina responded before Yogi Krishna Soham could.

"Because," Kurt explained, "there could come a time when the three conditions for truth don't align. Let's say for example that you are being chased by a terrorist with an assault weapon and I see you hide in a closet. If the terrorist then asks me where you are, should I tell him the truth? No. That would not promote beauty or happiness or be good for all."

"It is easy to distort these principles by playing philosophical mind games," Yogi Krishna Soham said, trying to quell the argument, "so let me repeat what I stated in the beginning. These ethical principles may influence how you behave towards other people, but their primary purpose is to create internal harmony — never forget that."

"I just took the terrorist example because that is a very real threat to our society," Kurt tried to explain. However, as he looked around and saw the displeasure his nitpicking was creating, he quickly ditched his effort. "But I understand what you are saying," he continued. "The yamas and niyamas are meant to guide the yoga practitioner — not to create a perfect world, right?"

Yogi Krishna Soham gave Kurt a civil smile and a nod for backing down.

"The next two principles are tightly linked," Yogi Krishna Soham continued, turning his attention to the rest of the group. "Aparigraha is non-greediness, and asteya is non-stealing. If the mind of the yoga practitioner is continually grasping and wanting things that other people have, then the practitioner is distracted from his goal of unveiling that which does not change. The difficult question to ask oneself is, how much is enough, then stop acquiring things, wanting things, when that mark is reached."

"Isn't it natural for people to want things, to want to improve their position in life?" Edna, the lawyer from New Jersey, asked.

"Of course. All of the animal instincts are completely natural. That is why adhering to the yamas and niyamas is hard work. If violence, lying, grasping, stealing and sexuality were not already parts of our physical and psychological makeup, then there would be no need for the yamas and niyamas."

"Don't tell me that you are about to demonize sexuality," Stacey blurted out in protest.

"My dear miss Stacey," Yogi Krishna Soham responded gracefully. "Demonizing sexuality and seeing it for what it is are two utterly different things. Sexuality is a powerful evolutionary driving force that is deeply embedded in human beings. The fifth yama or refraining principle, namely brahmacharya, refers to harnessing the sexual energy and funneling it towards the divine, the Atman within, that which does not change. Traditionally, brahmacharya has been translated as abstinence or chastity, but when you delve deeper and look at the meaning of the words—charya means devotion and brahma means God or absolute reality — then you see that the goal of abstaining from physical sex is about controlling energy, not repressing it."

"But, you are still saying that physical sex is bad," Stacey responded, allowing her unexpressed resentments about the dress code to surface.

"No," Yogi Krishna Soham replied quite adamantly. "I am saying that sex is a distraction to anyone who wants to unveil the Atman, to experience directly that which does not change. If you do not want that, feel free to have all the sex you want."

"I am sorry, Yogi Krishna," Andrea said, "but I can't get over what you are saying. Are you telling us that you and Lilavati never, ever...?" She realized what she was about to ask him and immediately tried to back out. "I'm sorry, Yogi Krishna. I crossed the line. That's none of my business."

"It's quite alright, miss Andrea," Yogi Krishna Soham answered with a laugh. "Why do you think I have so much energy at sixty-five? It's a combination of abstinence, diet, exercise and meditation, but we haven't been abstinent from the beginning, we have kids after all. You see, step one in rising above the pull of sexual energy is to become monogamous. Then, with time, Lilavati and I realized how distracting sex could be. We have willfully abstained from it for almost twenty years now. It has not lessened our love for each other, rather increased it if anything. We both enjoy more energy and fewer distractions as a result."

The group was stunned. No one knew how to respond to this personal admission.

"Your response is no different from any other group I have taught," Yogi Krishna Soham continued. "Everyone thinks that denial of sexuality is the ultimate repression, fostered by the belief that sexuality is a central human necessity. After all, sex is a vital part of our genetic animal programming. We are programmed to focus on sex, to procreate, to multiply. After we finish our procreation duties, however, there is no need for sex, except for pleasure and enjoyment."

No one was writing. Several mouths were open.

"The enjoyment of sex pales in comparison to the joy of being submerged in the experience of the Atman. That is what I have been trying to tell you all along. That is what all the masters have been trying to tell humanity. Let go of the animal sensory pleasures and experience true bliss and happiness. Only the self, the soul, the Atman, that which does not change can deliver unconditional happiness. Only that provides us with the deep internal peace and serenity that we all long for. Sex, or any other sensory stimulation for that matter, pales in comparison."

Yogi Krishna Soham looked over the group, searching for signs of comprehension. He waited patiently to see if there were any questions.

"Since there are no questions, let us now turn our attention to the niyamas or positive qualities that the yoga practitioner should acquire—"

Yogi Krishna Soham stopped when a familiar hand went up. "Yes, BJ?"

"I am sorry, Yogi Krishna, but I am still trying to wrap my head around what you just said," BJ replied, "and it looks like I am not the only one," he added, looking around the room. "I wonder, though, I mean, isn't all this suppression kind of dangerous? When I look at societies that quell sensory pleasure, forbid dancing, extramarital sex, alcohol and so on, I see societies that are very unforgiving, violent and dangerous even. Look at what the Spanish Inquisition did, for example. Look at what has been done in the name of Allah by people who are pious when it comes to their own living. In contrast, I don't see many individuals, who are sexually satisfied and enjoy a drink every now and then, behave in a violent manner that comes close to the viciousness shown by those who deny or repress pleasures of the flesh."

"I have to agree with BJ's assessment, Yogi Krishna," Kurt chimed in. "I have been studying the social standings of mass shooters in the USA, who have mostly been isolated men. Some of my peers have suggested that if they got laid every now and then, it might stifle their violence and rage. I just can't see how sex could be so wrong. It's generally accepted as good for procreation, pleasure, and tension relief."

"That's just typical of you men," Stacey responded before Yogi Krishna could get a word in. "Always ready to jump into any conversation that revolves around sex, always trying to defend the fact that you can't keep it in your pants."

"That's not fair Stacey," BJ replied.

"Enough!" Yogi Krishna Soham thundered.

The room went silent.

"See!" Yogi Krishna Soham then said with a smile. "Sex is a distraction. It riles up feelings of passion, distrust, disgust, and lust.

Let me repeat. Those who do not seek to uncover that which does not change can have all the sex they want. Those who seek to unveil the eternal Atman, however, will do well to reduce their sexual interactions or abstain from sex completely. Their goal should be to funnel their energy towards the divine. To address your concern BJ, anyone who abstains from sex and drugs should also follow the other principles, including non-violence."

"It sounds like a tall order, Yogi Krishna," BJ replied. "Even if I were to only follow the five principles you just laid out, I can see myself stumbling over and over again."

"That is why yoga is not for everyone," Yogi Krishna Soham replied. "For the dedicated yogi or yogini, these disciplines create boundless freedom, remove obstacles and open the door to that which does not change. Without that understanding, the yamas become chains, burdens that suck all the joy out of life. With understanding, however, the yamas provide a gateway to real and permanent happiness."

"I only see restrictions, things that I shouldn't do," BJ said resignedly, "which probably means that I have a long way to go."

"That is why we call it a practice, not a destination," Yogi Krishna Soham explained. "The dedication is to continuous improvement, to refining the physical, energetic, emotional and mental pathways in order for that which does not change to shine through. One part of that equation is subduing animal tendencies. Another is reinforcing positive qualities. The five niyamas represent the flip side of the coin."

"I guess I can never be a real yogi then," Kurt whispered in BJ's ear.

"Me neither," BJ whispered back with exasperation.

"What are the two of you whispering about?" Yogi Krishna Soham queried.

"We just said that we will never be real yogis," BJ replied.

"Never say never," Yogi Krishna Soham stated. "You may feel that way now, just as when you were children and said that you never wanted to stop playing with your action figures or video games. Then, one day, you realized that they had served their purpose, and you moved on. The same is true when working with these disciplines. Sooner or later you realize that certain behaviors no longer serve a purpose. There is no hurry. You have only just begun the real practice of yoga. If you continue to pursue this path, who knows what will happen."

Chapter Thirteen

"He hasn't had sex with his wife for almost twenty years," Sara asked in utter disbelief, "and they are still together? Why? How? What are they thinking?"

"It seems to be what they have chosen to do," BJ replied, pushing the payphone receiver—which he had previously rubbed with sanitizer—up against his ear while cupping his other ear with the palm of his other hand to reduce traffic sounds.

"I understand religious monogamy, really, I do," Sara continued, "but I thought celibacy was reserved for monks and nuns. Why do they stay married if there is no sex?"

"That's not really a good argument, is it?" BJ countered. "Relationships have other dimensions than sex."

"Sure, but from what you have told me, it sounds like Yogi Krishna's wife is his servant more than anything else. She cooks for him, cleans for him—when she is not having you guys do it—and bows to him like he was her master."

"I've been around Lilavati, Sara, and she may be reserved, but she is no servant. I guess they have just chosen to live like this. Who are we to judge?"

"You're right, but a relationship without sex for twenty years? I can't imagine it."

"Nor can I," BJ said, "but I am beginning to understand some of the reasoning."

"Don't you dare tell me that you are coming home a monk, Bjarni."

"No, I wouldn't dream of it, but I understand that sex takes up a lot of space in a person's life. Single or married, it demands a great deal of energy."

"And provides a great deal of joy."

"That it does."

"I miss you, Bjarni. I can't believe that I will have to spend three more weeks without you."

"I miss you too."

"Feel free to practice this celibacy thing while you are there, but once you come home—"

"I'm all yours. I promise."

"Do you think it's real, though, that they haven't had sex in twenty years?"

"My roommate, the psychologist, believes that there is something fishy going on, but I don't know if I can trust his instincts on this. He has a very active libido, and I think that it sometimes clouds his judgment."

"Tell me, though," Sara queried, "what did he say?"

"He said that Yogi Krishna and Lilavati look like some of the couples he has counseled over the years. She is fat and introverted while he is fit and extroverted. In such cases, Kurt says that the man is usually having an affair."

"I can see how that could be true."

"Yeah, maybe in our culture, but I choose to believe him, Sara. He may be a little over the top sometimes, but I think that he is, at the very least, trustworthy, a man of his word."

"Either way, it's probably none of our business, is it?"

"Probably not."

There was a moment of silence. Neither of them knew where to take the conversation next. BJ moved the payphone receiver from one ear, which felt numb after twenty minutes of talking, to the other.

"How do you feel about teaching tomorrow?" Sara finally asked.

"I feel alright," BJ replied, "although probably not as ready as I thought I was. Thomas taught this morning, and we all thought he did a great job, but Govinda chewed him out. Evidently none of us got the memo that we should teach the exact routine that Yogi Krishna has been leading us through twice a day."

"Really? But isn't Thomas a seasoned yoga teacher? He's the one who owns the yoga studio in Colorado, right?"

"Yeah, as I said, we all thought he did really well, and Govinda commended him for his confidence, but then he went after his routine with a vengeance. Thomas handled it well enough, he is mature for his age, but it rattled the rest of us."

"You're going to be alright. You know the routine by heart, don't you?"

"I think so, but we'll see tomorrow."

"Promise to call me when you're done."

"When have I ever not called?" BJ replied, thinking about how he'd made the trek to the payphone every day, rain or shine.

"Never," she replied, "but it's fun to make you promise."

BJ could hear her smile through the phone. She loved to tease him. He truly missed her.

"I have to go now. Two more people are teaching this afternoon, and they expect all of us to be there for it. Also, I have to brush up on my routine."

"Talk to you tomorrow."

"Love you. Bye."

BJ hung up the phone, swung by Subway for his daily dose of meat and started walking back, eating the sub on the way. The weather was bearable, overcast with temperatures in the low eighties, and there was no rain in the forecast. BJ was only sweating moderately when he came upon the ashram gravel driveway. Kicking up dust in every step, he stayed in the center of the road, just as he had done the first day, still not over his fear of insects and snakes. The chirping and rattling sounds were unusually loud in the still air. When he entered the parking lot, he saw Andrea walking briskly towards him.

"Have you heard?" she yelled.

"Heard what?"

"They were expelled. Stacey and Ang Lin. They just left. Govinda expelled them from the program. No second chance. No refund. They're gone. I am so angry that I might explode."

"Did he find out about the sex and drugs?" BJ asked.

"Little miss Blossom developed a conscience after last night's lecture about the yamas and niyamas and told Govinda everything."

"You can't blame her, Andrea. It's not fair to ask her to lie. She's nineteen for goodness sake. Stacey and Ang Lin knew the rules but chose to ignore them. You shouldn't fault the messenger."

"You're not angry?"

"Why should I be?"

"Because — everyone else is angry. This is an outrage!"

"No, it isn't. We all entered into an agreement when we chose to attend this program. Stacey and Ang Lin violated that agreement. That's all that happened."

"Oh, so you think its just business as usual?"

"This is how the real world works, Andrea. I deal with this kind of stuff all the time, not the sex and drugs part, but enforcing contracts. I own several rental spaces and have had to evict my fair share of tenants. There is no room for emotions when one is enforcing a contract. Everyone needs to calm down."

"Good luck with that," Andrea replied, still fuming.

"Come now, Andrea. We have to keep calm."

Andrea shook her head in protest.

"What's going on guys," Govinda shouted from a distance. He was returning from a walk with Lulu.

"I think we need to join forces and calm the group," BJ replied. "It seems like you caused quite a ruckus by expelling Stacey and Ang Lin from the program."

"They broke the rules," Govinda replied.

"I know," BJ said, "and I am on your side, but you need to deal with flaring tempers before the situation gets out of hand."

Chapter Fourteen

"You're up BJ."

It was Friday and BJ was about to teach his very first yoga class. He was more nervous than he'd expected. Also, it was clear that dealing with the outrage alongside Govinda the day before had taken a toll. Upon entering the sleeping quarters, after hearing about the expulsion, BJ and Govinda had walked into a chattering group of infuriated women.

Laurie had thought Govinda was being mean, Edna had wanted him to find middle ground, Jasmine had been appalled, Poppy had seen the expulsion as too strict, and Valentina had said that this course of action was decidedly unspiritual. The other women had stood with them in solidarity while Thomas and Kurt had stayed away from the argument.

Eventually, the women had agreed to listen to BJ's reasoning and with the help of Betsy, who'd been the only woman who was not up in arms about the whole thing, the group had calmed down.

The ordeal had taken almost half the day.

BJ had then spent Thursday night going through the yoga routine over and over again, both in his head and on paper. Now, he sat cross-legged on the knee-high stage — which felt taller than he'd expected — and was about to do something he had never done before.

"Let us begin by chanting Aum together," he said, his voice cracking slightly.

He steadied himself, took a deep breath and started chanting, but he didn't hit the note he wanted to. The sound coming from his throat was wobbly and too low, but, instead of beginning again, he persisted. The group tried to follow along, but the pitch was unclear. The attempt created a disharmony unlike any other heard during their time at the ashram. Three times in a row that happened. BJ struck a sour note, and the group did its best to follow. When BJ opened his eyes, he tried to shake off the vibrations. The cacophony of sounds had distracted him. He stood up and positioned himself at the front of his yoga mat, expecting the rest of the group to do the same, but he hadn't spoken, so no one moved.

"Please stand up and come to the front of your mat," he said.

The group complied.

BJ wanted to emulate Yogi Krishna Soham's minimalistic teaching style, using the fewest number of words possible. It started well. The sun salutations flowed.

"Inhale, stretch up, exhale, bend forward, inhale, right leg back, hold the breath and step back into the plank, exhale, staff pose, inhale, upward dog, exhale, downward dog..."

A few rounds into the class, BJ realized that Thomas had been right. Combining words and movement was much harder than it seemed to be, and yet, he did it. He remembered the right words at the right time, even managed to lead the group through several variations of the posture combination. He was on a roll until it came time to stop doing the sun salutations. At that point, he froze, unsure of what to do next. His mind went blank. He looked at the group with the sophistication of a deer caught in the headlights. He was embarrassed.

"I... I..." he stuttered, completely unlike his usual confident and rational self.

He was the engine that was supposed to pull the train, but as he stood still, so did the cars. The group stood motionless, looking more like an ancient Chinese clay army than a band of yoga students.

The silence was deafening.

"Headstand preparation," Laurie finally whispered.

"Oh, yes, headstand preparation," BJ replied, giving her the nod. "Come down onto your hands and knees, then on your elbows, grab the outsides of the upper arms..."

And just like that, he was back on a roll.

After BJ had brought the group out of relaxation, Govinda began giving feedback.

"What happened after the sun salutations?" he asked.

"I froze," BJ replied. "I had no idea what to do next."

"And how did that feel?"

"It was a feeling of helplessness and embarrassment that I haven't felt since I was in my teens," BJ replied. "I felt completely out of my element. If Laurie hadn't—"

"She shouldn't have done that," Govinda interrupted.

"Why?" both Laurie and BJ replied.

"Because that will never happen in real life. None of your students will ever help you. They are there to get guidance from you, not the other way around. If you ever freeze again, you will need to figure it out on your own."

"That's a good point," BJ replied.

"Other than that, you did well," Govinda continued. "What did you think guys?"

"I believe he did a great job," Kurt said.

BJ couldn't decipher whether or not Kurt was being sarcastic.

"Yes, good job, guy from Iceland," Laurie added with a smile, then proposed a toast with her water bottle.

"Be serious," Govinda interjected, "and tell him what you liked and what he can do better next time."

"I liked how to the point you were," Valentina offered, seemingly showing off her perfect posture by the way she carried herself, "but maybe next time you could give more detailed descriptions, perhaps even inject some feeling."

"No, I really liked it. To the point. Physical. No need for poetry, right?" Poppy, the aerobics teacher, said.

"I think that yoga should make the students feel good," Valentina countered, "and I believe that encouraging people to feel more, for example, by using poetic imagery, achieves exactly that."

"I'm sorry," BJ responded, now sitting with his feet off the stage, "but I am not a touchy feely guy. I don't think I could ever do that."

"You could try," Valentina pressed, "maybe you just need to get in touch with your own feelings first."

"What do you say to that, Govinda?" BJ asked.

"What is the goal of yoga according to Gurudev?" the Swiss man replied with a question.

"To uncover that which does not change," the young Blossom replied instantly.

"Exactly," Govinda replied. "Do emotions stay the same or change?"

"They change," the group replied.

"Then the question is, does focusing on emotions bring us closer to the goal of yoga or further away from it?"

All of them knew the answer, but nobody said it out loud.

"But people are so out of touch with their bodies and their emotions," Valentina responded after a moment of silence, once again forced to defend her point of view. "Can't focusing on emotions be a stepping stone towards unveiling that which does not change?"

"I think there are two different concepts at play here, Valentina," Kurt interceded from where he sat on three pillows up against the wall. "Firstly, you talk about encouraging people to feel a certain way. That requires visualization, imagination, projection. People have to imagine that they feel a certain way. Although such an approach can be helpful psychologically, I don't think that it helps the practitioner uncover that which does not change."

"That may be so, but when people feel good, they come back to class," Valentina countered. "I know that the end goal of yoga is to uncover that which does not change, but let's be real for a moment. If you work as a yoga teacher, as I have done, you need to make money, and part of that is getting people to come back."

"What's concept number two?" BJ asked, ignoring Valentina's counter argument.

"Well, as I see it, the other concept is mindfulness, focusing intently on whatever arises from moment to moment," Kurt explained, "be that your thoughts, emotions or physical sensations. Observing it all with detachment. That should help the practitioner uncover that which does not change, right Govinda?"

"Gurudev says that there is a tremendous difference between imagination and pure awareness," Govinda replied, "so I would agree with your assessment. But we need to keep going, guys. Anyone want to give BJ more feedback on his performance?"

"Yes, I'd like to say a few words," Edna, the lawyer, chimed in. "I don't know if you are going to be teaching much in Iceland BJ, seeing as you probably won't abandon your job as an investor, but you have a genuine presence. I liked your class. I would come on a regular basis if I lived in Iceland. I hope that people there will appreciate your rational, to the point, and even-keeled approach."

"Thank you, Edna," BJ replied.

He had not expected such a comment.

"Okay, if nobody else is going to say it, then I will," Andrea interjected as she sat up and put aside the pillows she had been lying on top of. "I think that Valentina has voiced a concern that many of us have been thinking about over the past two weeks. This idea of that which does not change is all well and good, but yoga is also a business, and I don't see how yoga teachers can sell 'nothing' to Americans. You may say that the 'touchy feely' stuff is not very yogic, but as Valentina pointed out, in many cases that, along with the fitness aspect, is what keeps people coming back."

"And pain," Laurie added. "I just read an article about the founder of hot yoga. He finishes every teacher training by telling his trainees to go out and make people feel pain. The more pain they feel, he says, the more they will pay you. That doesn't sound very yogic either, but it seems to capture the essence of Western psychology, the idea of no pain, no gain."

"Sounds about right," Kurt replied with a sigh. "How would you answer that Govinda?"

"Look, guys," Govinda proceeded, "Gurudev is painfully aware of all the challenges that yoga teachers face in the modern world. He knows about the marketing elements and how seductive it can be to alter yoga to fit the psychology of the masses, but he has decided to go against the grain and stay true to the core teachings of yoga. As graduates of his program, you are welcome to teach yoga partially, only teach physical posture and relaxation if that is what you want to do. In fact, he knows that he cannot control what you do once you leave here, but during this training he wants to make sure that you understand that intention matters. Internally directed awareness leads to yoga while externally directed awareness leads to confusion."

Govinda was clearly frustrated. He paused to take a deep breath before he continued.

"I understand your concerns, really, I do guys, but there are plenty of courses on marketing out there. At the same time, there are not so many who teach the essence of yoga. Even if you are somewhat confused now, consider yourselves lucky to have access to a program like this."

No one spoke up, even though there was more to be said.

"It's almost eleven o'clock, Govinda," BJ said, wanting to end this conversation, for now, wanting to shake off the tension after going through his first teaching session. "Isn't it time for seva. I could use some gardening to clear my mind right about now."

"Yes," Govinda replied, thankful for their newfound camaraderie. "Let's do our work, then take a break and meet here for Andrea's class at two in the afternoon."

Before Govinda could say Namaste and dismiss the class, Lilavati appeared in the doorway and pointed towards him. He told the group to stay put for a moment and walked over to her. She whispered in his ear, and he looked up with an expression of grave concern on his face.

"BJ," Govinda called. "Lilavati tells me that your mother is on the phone. It's an emergency."

BJ jumped off the stage and ran over to Lilavati. She walked in front of him, too slowly for his taste, leading him step by step over to the orange cottage. Upon entering the building, BJ was greeted with a strong smell of incense. The foyer was colorful but sparsely decorated. A corded phone stood on a table next to the front door, and the receiver lay on the table beside it. Lilavati pointed to the phone and BJ picked it up hastily.

"Mom," he said with worry in his voice, "is everything okay?"

"No Bjarni," she answered.

He could tell that she had been crying.

"Your father is in the hospital."

Hospitalized with a bleeding ulcer, that's what had happened to BJ's dad. Upon hearing the news, the Icelandic investor was overcome with feelings of absolute helplessness, because, instead of being by his father's side, he was stuck in the Florida dampness during the middle of summer.

Chapter Fifteen

The night after hearing the news, which was also the night before the two hundred hour graduation ceremony, BJ sat motionless in the common area of the sleeping quarters, observing his fellow students interact in a way that they hadn't done before. An hour earlier, they had concluded their written examination, and now everyone was giddy as if they had ingested a controlled substance of some kind. The chattering was constant. BJ observed dispassionately, like a fly on the wall. He felt numb.

His roommate, the young Thomas, was in a deep conversation with Edna, the lawyer, Laurie, the cowgirl, and Valentina, the Anusara yoga teacher, about his plans for his yoga studio. They sat in a corner underneath the staircase and talked about how to balance authentic yoga with marketing needs. Above them hung a framed picture of a lotus flower. Thomas and Valentina seemed at odds, although the discussion was mostly agreeable. He was on the side of authentic yoga while she was trying to explain how it was necessary to meet the demands of the market by catering to feelings and fitness needs. Edna seemed to be somewhere in the middle, her law degree and arbitration skills shining through.

The German ladies, Malin, and Gerwalta were engaged in a conversation about animal rights and veganism with Camille and Kurt, getting some pushback from Andrea, who ate her meat unabashedly. BJ couldn't tell if Andrea was actually defending her meat eating habits or just yanking their chain. She reminded him of his father, who would often take an opposing view just to see if the other person would stick to his or her conviction. If the other person gave up too quickly, he would chide them for not sticking to their guns.

The most interesting conversation that BJ could overhear was an exchange of words between old lady Betsy Brigham and Jasmine, the belly dancer, both of whom sat across from BJ on a pile of purple, orange and yellow pillows. Betsy was explaining to Jasmine, who was hugging one of the pillows to her chest, how she used to live in a commune in the early seventies and how, even though everyone was supposed to be equal, sex was consistently used as a way to control others. BJ was intrigued by her description of power moves, seemingly Machiavellian in nature, mostly administered by the women. Despite their longing for no possessions and no leaders, the commune had been brimming with political tension. Sex had been the weapon of choice. The commune had finally broken up due to jealousy and general animosity. Betsy had reverted back to her Christian values and had never longed for those days again. To BJ, it sounded as if the older lady was trying to caution the young belly dancer about the explosiveness of using sexuality as a mechanism for money and power. Jasmine looked both intrigued and confused. BJ wondered if she understood everything that Betsy was saying — linguistically, that is.

BJ's reverie was interrupted when Poppy, the aerobics teacher, sat next to him and whispered tentatively: "Are you okay? I heard about your father."

Looking at Poppy, BJ noticed that she was genuinely concerned.

"I don't know," BJ replied. "I don't know how I feel."

"How is your father doing?"

"He's better, I think. I spent my entire lunch hour on the phone, both talking to my girlfriend and my mother, but all they could tell me was that he is stable."

Poppy nodded empathetically.

"I just wish I could see him and talk to him," BJ continued. "I wish we didn't have this stupid electronics ban here at the ashram. I feel so… so… helpless…"

"I understand," Poppy replied. She had tears in her eyes. "I was halfway across the country at an aerobics convention when my mother died earlier this year. I felt completely helpless."

"She died? I am so sorry to hear that," BJ heard himself say with an unusual amount of emotion in his voice. "Is that why you've been crying," he added, not realizing that he was repeating gossip from Andrea. His natural ability to self-censor had evidently been weakened by the shock of his father's illness.

Poppy chuckled to herself, tears still in her eyes.

"Has it been that obvious?"

"No, no, I mean—"

"Don't worry about it, BJ," she replied. "I have been trying to keep it from all of you, putting on my peppy aerobics mask. Poppy is always peppy," she said, tilting her head and giving her best fake smile. "I guess I didn't fool anyone—except myself, maybe."

"No, when somebody dies it's personal," BJ said. "You are not obligated to share your pain."

"True, but oddly enough, I feel better for having told you about my mother's passing. You're the first one in this training I have trusted with that information."

"Thank you."

"You're welcome."

They turned away from each other momentarily and allowed the chatter from the rest of the group to fill the void. When their eyes met again, BJ had teared up as well. He was surprised by the empathy effect, especially since he hadn't cried since he was a teenager.

As the two of them cried silently, a hush came over the room. BJ looked up and saw that everyone was looking at them and the natural waterfalls that were flowing down their cheeks. The room erupted into oohs and aahs. After learning that Poppy's mother had died, most of the women rushed to her side to give her hugs. She let go of her mask completely and cried without restraint.

BJ moved away while she was being consoled. As he did, Valentina turned to him and said: "Would you like a healing session, BJ? You look like you need it."

BJ did not believe in any of the New Age stuff that had been so prevalent in the nineties and early two thousands. In the past, if anyone mentioned astrology, healing, reiki, or shamanism, he hadn't been content letting it go with a shoulder shrug, rather, he'd gone after such a person with all the tools in his rational toolbox. He had repeatedly decimated well-meaning women who had been trying to make him feel better.

Would he like a healing session? He was overwhelmed by a feeling of helplessness, had tears running down his cheeks for the first time since he was in his teens, felt a knot in the pit of his stomach, and a growing void in his heart. Would he like a healing session?

"Yes, please," BJ finally replied in a broken voice.

Valentina ushered him to the other side of the room, had him lie down on the floor, arranged pillows under his head and knees, and knelt beside him. She told him to close his eyes and placed one hand a few inches over his abdomen and another hand over his heart. BJ complied with her instructions. With his eyes closed, he could hear Poppy whimper and the women try to comfort her. His body felt stiff, his emotions —

"Now, take a few deep breaths," Valentina suggested.

Having practiced breathing techniques for a half an hour every day for the past few weeks, breathing deeply was easy for BJ to do. However, when he exhaled after taking the deepest breath he could muster, he realized that he hadn't actually taken a deep breath since he'd heard about his father's condition the day before. He immediately felt better.

"Good," Valentina urged him on. "Continue breathing deeply."

He did. Within two minutes, he felt lightheaded and returned his breathing to a steady pace. Valentina kept her hands in place over his abdomen and heart, and, as strange as it seemed, BJ could sense exactly where her hands were, almost like there was a slight current of electricity connecting her skin to his. The sensation grew stronger and within a few minutes, BJ felt a deepening sense of warmth around his heart and in his abdomen. The feeling was so comforting that he relaxed completely, withdrew his consciousness and lost track of time.

"BJ? BJ?"

Valentina gently nudged him, and BJ opened his eyes. He looked around. The room was empty, except for the two of them.

"What happened?"

"You fell asleep. It often happens during these healing sessions."

BJ felt revitalized and energized. Emotional turmoil had left him for now and been replaced with a profound sense of calm. He had been healed.

"Thank you, Valentina," he said. "I've ridiculed this healing stuff so often, I—"

"I know," she replied in a soothing tone. "I know."

She smiled. BJ looked deeply into her green eyes, felt her energy, and shared her emotions. The connection between them was so intense that he would have allowed himself to fall in love—if not for the fact that he was in a committed relationship.

"Now go to bed," she said, somehow picking up on his romantic musings. "We have a big day tomorrow. Our first graduation ceremony."

Chapter Sixteen

The graduation ceremony for the two hundred hour accreditation began at ten o'clock sharp on a beautiful Sunday morning. It had rained earlier, which meant that the sun hadn't gotten a chance to warm the air to its usual muggy temperature. It was the closest to crisp the air had been since the training began.

The setup in the yoga hall was similar to Satsang, with plenty of candles and flowers. In addition, flower petals had been strewn artistically around the room and a petal path constructed from the middle of the room to the stage where Yogi Krishna Soham would be sitting. Each and every teacher trainee was dressed in white or off-white clothing. The ashram had gotten a shipment of cheap hemp and cotton clothing from India earlier that week. Those who had not previously owned white garbs were out of excuses.

In addition to the teacher trainees, three of Yogi Krishna Soham's disciples were in attendance; the curly-haired Alyssa Floros, who Yogi Krishna called Sunita, the overly devoted Patricia Erhardt, who Yogi Krishna had renamed Rukmini, and the writer Tiffany Rotrosen, who reluctantly bore the name Sucheta.

The group chanted Om Namo Bhagavate Vasudevaya as Yogi Krishna Soham entered the room in his finest white garbs, hair and beard combed and trimmed, sandalwood mala beads hanging around his neck, his hands in prayer position, his eyes half closed. He walked slowly towards the stage and sat down in a full lotus pose. The singing stopped. He greeted the group warmly.

"Namaste!" he said.

"Namaste!" the group replied in concert.

"This is a most auspicious occasion," the yoga master continued. "Sucheta, Rukmini, Sunita," he said, bowing to each of the women, "thank you for joining us during this most sacred ceremony."

The three ladies bowed their heads in response, each saying:

"Namaste, Gurudev."

Yogi Krishna Soham then took the time to recognize each of the students with a smile and a nod, just as he had done at the beginning of the training two weeks earlier.

"Many of you think that you will be receiving a fitness instructor certificate here today," he finally said. "Nothing could be further from the truth. You are being initiated into a line of authentic yoga teachers that originated in India thousands of years ago. It is because of the grace of my guru, Swamidev, that we are gathered here today, able to spread original teachings of yoga with understanding and empathy. By finishing the two hundred hour course, you have taken a valiant first step towards enlightenment and shown the willingness to devote your lives to serving others. The great yoga master, Swami Sivananda, said these words of wisdom: Serve. Love. Give. Purify. Meditate. Realize."

Yogi Krishna Soham took his signature pause to let the words sink in.

"He said, serve, love, and give—not be greedy, show off, and take. Serve, love, and give! Commit those words to memory. Think of them often. Apply them to your teaching. They are your guiding light when interacting with others."

The trainees sat in complete stillness, nodding their heads slightly in response to his words.

"Purify, meditate, and realize. Those words are directed towards your own personal practice. Purify, meditate, and realize. Find your well within, connect deeply with that which does not change, and you will never have to depend on external sources for your happiness again. Your bliss will come from the inside."

Yogi Krishna Soham placed his hands on his heart.

"Atman is the source of joy, the source of love, the source of bliss. The Buddha was right when he pointed out that life is suffering. If you look for happiness externally, it will cause you pain, eventually. Everything on the outside changes and will degenerate, end, die, transform. The world changes, but in real yoga we uncover—"

" — that which does not change," the group responded in chorus and on cue.

"Excellent! Excellent!" Yogi Krishna Soham shouted, clapping his hands. "We are ready to begin the ceremony. Miss Blossom."

"Yes, Yogi Krishna Soham."

"Please come to the front of the stage."

The nineteen-year-old Blossom held her head high as she walked to the stage, wearing a beautiful knee-length white dress and white tie-pants with her curly hair in a bun. Once there, she knelt in front of Yogi Krishna Soham. He blessed her, rubbed a red dot on the center of her forehead, and presented her with a certificate of completion. When she received warm applause from the group, her cheeks turned rosier than usual.

The procession continued, each of the thirteen remaining students came to the front of the stage, bowed, received a red dot on their forehead, and walked back to their seat with a certificate in hand. The three lady guests, plus Govinda and Lilavati, also came to the front of the stage to receive a blessing and a red dot on their foreheads.

After the ceremony, the students walked around the room congratulating each other, saying goodbye to the six women who were leaving at noon.

Camille Lundgren, from Sweden, stepped up to BJ and congratulated him.

"Thank you," he responded. "Grattis."

"Oh, congratulations in Swedish?" she responded, looking surprised.

"Yeah, we learn Danish in school in Iceland. With it comes a smattering of Swedish and Norwegian."

"We probably should have connected earlier in the training," she said.

"Probably."

BJ knew why they hadn't. It was self-preservation on his part. With her soft features, blonde hair and blue eyes, Camille was exactly the kind of woman that BJ had fallen for in the past. She reminded him of a younger version of his ex, Hafdís.

"I was sad to hear about your dad."

"Tack så mycket."

"Du är välkommen."

"That's about all I know in Swedish."

Camille smiled. BJ didn't know what else to say. There was an awkward silence. He was about to move on when she leaned in and whispered: "I don't know whether to tell you this, but I think Yogi Krishna Soham is having an affair with that woman who writes for him."

"What?" BJ responded, then whispered: "You think he's having an affair with Tiffany?"

"Yes, I saw him hug her for a long time the other day, and I see how he looks at her when she comes to lectures and classes."

"A hug and a look? That's what you are basing your assumptions on?"

"I just thought that you should know since you will be here for three more weeks."

"Thanks, but I wish you hadn't told me."

"I like Yogi Krishna, but I definitely think that something is going on," she pressed gently. "You should keep your eyes open."

"Even if he is having an affair — which I don't believe he is, not based solely on what you just told me — why should I care?"

"Because of what he teaches, telling us to have no sex."

"He didn't say not to have sex, Camille. He said that if we truly want to unveil that which does not change, then giving up sex might help us achieve that."

"You are upset," she said. "I just wanted to tell you my suspicions, because you are my friend from Scandinavia."

"That's okay," BJ replied and took a deep breath. "I overreacted. I am a little stressed because of my dad."

"I hope he feels better."

"Me too."

"Tack."

"Adjö. Have a safe trip home."

BJ decided to keep Camille's gossip to himself and walked around the hall receiving congratulations from all the women and robust hugs from Thomas and Kurt, the latter being exceptionally proud of his own achievement.

"I am going to get off the premises and call my wife once this ceremony is done," Kurt said, beaming with pride. "There is no class until this evening when the advanced training begins. I gather that Yogi Krishna Soham and Lilavati are going to the movies this afternoon."

"They are going to the movies?" BJ replied.

"Yeah."

BJ laughed and shook his head.

"You wanna hear something stupid?" he asked Kurt, then continued without waiting for an answer. "I just had to contend with my own prejudices when I heard that. For some reason, a part of me thought that the two of them, such spiritual creatures, didn't participate in Western society like that."

"You thought that they didn't go to the movies?"

"I know. It sounds strange when you say it out loud. Of course, they can go to the movies, right? But some part of me thought they didn't."

"That's the mind for you," Kurt replied. "Always making up stories to fit preconceived ideas and stereotypes."

"Guilty as charged," BJ said, raising his hands like he was under arrest.

"You wanna come with me?"

"No. Govinda found a mall that is in approximately forty minutes walking distance from here. I should be able to get on the Internet to call my dad there. Edna has lent me her smartphone so that I should be able to talk with him on Skype."

"Good luck with that. I'll see you tonight."

"Yeah, see you tonight, yoga teacher."

Kurt grinned proudly in response.

BJ was getting ready to leave when young Blossom tapped him on the back of the shoulder. She gave him a great big hug when he turned around.

"Thank you," she said after letting go of him.

"For what?"

"For standing up for me when I told on Stacey and Ang Lin."

"You are welcome. The two of them broke the rules. You were right to say something."

"It was a valuable lesson," she replied, her demeanor and tone indicating that she was an old spirit residing in a young body. "Honesty is hard. I won't forget it."

"The world will try to corrupt you at every turn, Blossom. Integrity is hard. Keep it up for as long as you can."

"I will. How is your dad?'

"They've stopped the bleeding. He is recovering. I get to see him on Skype later today."

"I hope he recovers."

"So do I."

Blossom threw her arms around BJ for another hug.

"Again, thank you."

Chapter Seventeen

After the ceremony, BJ and Kurt helped Blossom, Camille, Malin, Gerwalta, Jasmine, and Betsy, haul their luggage down the gravel driveway. After the six women had been picked up by a shuttle service at the curb, BJ headed in the opposite direction to where he usually went, armed only with a printout from Google maps and Edna's smartphone, which had no data package, making it useless as a guiding device. He was headed for the mall because he wanted to see his father face to face.

The crispness that had graced them with its presence that morning had made way for a familiar fog-like humidity. BJ could not determine whether he was sweating profusely or being bathed. Either way, he was wet from top to bottom.

Twenty minutes into the walk, BJ found himself at a three-story highway intersection. It took him a few moments to get his bearings and thread his way to the opposite corner of the street. Once there, he found no sidewalk. He chose to walk on the shoulder of the access road, even with loud motor sounds and whooshing wind gusts from car after car that sped by, nearly clipping his elbow, rather than walk in the tall grass where he could possibly face attacks from unknown reptiles and insects. When he finally reached the mall parking lot, he felt like bending down and kissing the concrete. In Iceland, he was a nature lover, but here, the unfamiliarity continually scared him.

When he entered the mall, BJ was struck with two equally uncomfortable feelings.

First, he felt cold to the bone. The below seventy air conditioning temperatures, combined with the sweat that covered his body, quickly produced an overwhelming chilly sensation. Within a minute he'd started to shiver. Thankfully, the corner table in the coffee house he found was warmer than the hallways. As his clothes dried, BJ slowly recovered. The hot coffee also helped.

Second, and more surprisingly, BJ felt rattled by all the people. The commotion was in stark contrast with the seclusion at the ashram. It was jarring, even to him who usually enjoyed large crowds, even sought them out. Now, he huddled in the corner and felt as if everyone was too loud, too fast, too busy, too stressed.

Was that all it took, two weeks at an ashram to make him crowd shy? No, it was just the change of surroundings, a shock similar to what he'd felt during his first day at the ashram.

Internet. He took out the smartphone and found the wireless settings. Within a minute he was online. He looked up his girlfriend's Skype account through Edna's phone and called. Sara was a sight for sore eyes. BJ could see that she was at the hospital.

"Hi, honey. How are you?"

Her sweet voice and beautiful face almost made him cry.

"I'm okay. I miss you."

"I miss you too."

"Is dad awake? Can I talk to him?"

"Yes," Sara answered and started walking towards his room with her phone. "Congratulations on graduating as a yoga teacher," she added.

"Thanks. I don't feel very festive, though."

"I understand. I'll talk to you later. Here is your dad."

His father's condition was worse than he'd imagined. The usually red-cheeked and vigorous sea captain had lost a lot of weight. He looked pale and gaunt.

"Hi, dad. How are you?"

"What does it look like, Bjarni?"

"Not great."

"That's how I feel not great but they say I am getting better."

"That's good to hear. Do they know what happened?"

"Your mom told you. Bleeding ulcer."

"Yeah, I know, but do they know how it happened?"

"These kid doctors have all kinds of theories. Stress, alcohol, too much whale and shark meat."

"And you don't believe them?"

"You know I've never put much stock in doctors, Bjarni, especially not the young ones. Sure, they may know how to stitch a person up, but they know very little about staying healthy."

"You should at least listen to what they say, dad. You're not a spring lamb anymore, you know."

"Yeah, yeah. Enough about me. I'll be okay. When are you coming home? Aren't you about done with this yoga nonsense?"

"I've got three weeks left, then I'll be home."

"Three weeks? What can be so hard about teaching people how to stretch, Bjarni. We do Muller exercises every morning at the swimming pool after we swim twenty laps. It only took me two or three repetitions to learn the whole routine. This yoga nonsense can't be much harder than that."

"There is a little more to it, dad. I don't want to argue. I just wanted to see you. I am glad to hear that you are getting better."

"I'll be okay. It's you I am worried about. You run into a little money and what do you do? Get a younger girlfriend and go halfway across the world to learn yoga."

"Dad. Can we talk about my life choices later? Maybe when Sara isn't standing next to you?"

"Don't be so sensitive, Bjarni."

"Well, dad. I can see that the ulcer hasn't dampened your spirit."

"I've faced circumstances out at sea that were a thousand times more perilous. I am not going to be beaten by stomach problems, that's for sure."

"That's good to hear. I am glad to see that you are doing better. Can I talk to Sara now?"

"Here she is. Come home soon, Bjarni. Your kids miss you and so does your mom."

"I miss you too, dad."

Sara took the phone and walked out into the hallway.

"He doesn't mean anything by it," BJ tried to explain.

"It's okay," Sara replied, "we don't need his blessing."

"No, we don't. Thanks for looking after him, though."

"He is very pleasant to me when you are not around. Whether he likes it or not, I am part of this family now."

"That's the spirit. One more reason why I love you, Sara."

"I love you too. How are you holding up down there?"

"On one hand, I am doing great. My body has limbered up after practicing yoga every day, and I actually look forward to the second half of the teacher training. On the other hand, I feel bad about not being there for my dad."

"I understand, but you wouldn't be able to do anything for him even if you were here."

"I know that intellectually, but emotionally□"

"Emotionally? Can I expect a sensitive version of my man to return from the training in three weeks?"

"Maybe… is that okay?"

"Do you have to ask? Of course, that's okay. It's one of the reasons why I urged you to take the training in the first place, to get in touch with all aspects of your being."

"Yeah, this experience is affecting me in unexpected ways. My dad being sick just amplifies everything."

BJ and Sara kept talking for over an hour. During that time, BJ also got to speak with his mother for a few minutes and say goodbye to his father again. It felt good not to be in a hurry to get back to the ashram. The daily two-hour window for communications was narrow, to say the least.

It was almost five in the afternoon when BJ began his trek back to the ashram. The weather was still cloudy and muggy. When he arrived at the three-story highway intersection, it started raining. The crackling thunder was deafening, and the rain came down in buckets. BJ had rarely seen such a display. Coming down straight, in copious amounts, the rain bounced several inches off the street, at one point almost reaching knee-height. The lightning made the underpass look like a strobe-lit discotheque. The thunder made him cover his ears several times and shook him to the bone.

BJ stayed under the overpass for about half an hour, until the storm passed, and then jogged the rest of the way, skipping across puddles in a light drizzle. Dinner was being served when he arrived back at the ashram.

Chapter Eighteen

"Now we can really begin," Yogi Krishna Soham said when the group of eight remaining students had gathered in the yoga hall after dinner on Sunday night, along with Sunita, Tiffany, Lilavati, and Govinda.

"Tonight, I will expand on a yoga sutra that has mostly been overlooked by students and scholars alike, but first, let me ask you." He paused to look at the group. "What would you like to get out of this advanced portion of the teacher training?"

"I'll go first," Laurie said eagerly.

Her hair was wet, either after taking a shower or being out in the rain, and she was still wearing her white garbs from earlier in the day. As were most of the others, aside from BJ and Thomas, who had both reverted to their dark athletic attire.

"Go ahead, miss Laurie," Yogi Krishna Soham said and bowed his head.

"For one, I want to teach more. I really felt at home when I taught last week and want to expand on that. I also want to learn how to put together programs for different types of yoga students."

"Yes, yes. You will all teach more," Yogi Krishna Soham said, straightening his back while tightening his lotus pose by pulling gently on his ankles and bringing the back of each foot higher on the opposing thigh. "Our schedule will continue, similar to what it has been so far, but I will teach only the morning classes, maybe not even that sometimes. This means that the afternoon classes now belong to the eight of you. You will divide the time between yourselves, which should allow each of you to teach at least twice before the program is over."

This revelation was met with smiles and under the breath cheers.

"We will also cover how to set up classes for different types of students," Yogi Krishna Soham continued, "both of which should make you happy, miss Laurie. How about you, miss Poppy? What do you want to get out of the three hundred hour training?"

After her breakdown in the sleeping quarters the previous night, Poppy looked and sounded different. She wasn't wearing her traditional colorful athletic wear, nor was she wearing any makeup. Her bleached hair was undone, and her off-white hemp clothes looked one size too big. She looked as if she had dropped her mask, unveiling a vulnerable version of herself.

"I want to remain open," Poppy answered in a low voice. "I came here to learn physical exercises, but in two weeks I have learned more about myself than I have at any previous point in my life. I don't completely understand the philosophy, but I understand that the silence and lack of external stimuli have allowed me to get in touch with parts of me that I never knew. I'm not sure if it's the Atman you keep talking about, but now I am curious. I am looking forward to unveiling more aspects of myself in the coming weeks."

A smile spread across Yogi Krishna Soham's entire face.

"Know thyself," he said. "That is our motto here at the ashram. You have indeed made enormous progress, miss Poppy. I am proud to call you my student."

"Thank you, Yogi Krishna."

Looking around the room, it was evident that the others had not expected such a profound revelation from Poppy. They were stunned.

"I am having a similar experience," BJ confessed. "Going to the mall today made me realize how much I have been affected by external stimuli and how seldom I have taken the time to simply be with myself. Also, the raw emotions surrounding my father's illness have opened my eyes to aspects of myself that were hidden. Sure, I look forward to teaching more and learning more about the business of yoga, but I agree with Poppy. I am curious to see what else I will unveil in the next three weeks."

After a round of nods, the attention shifted to Andrea.

"Jeez, you guys are all so sincere. I hope we are not going to be crying every day for the rest of the program. I'm just getting used the physical labor around here."

Her comical delivery elicited several laughs.

"All joking aside, though, I guess I just look forward to learning more. I am trying to stay open to this experience as well."

The rest of the students echoed those sentiments and within twenty minutes everyone had spoken.

"I look forward to observing each and every one of you as you begin to unveil more of your eternal self in the coming weeks," Yogi Krishna Soham said in response to the sharing session. "Now, let us begin." He took a deep breath. "As you know, Sucheta and I are working on a new book titled *The Spiritual Heritage of Yoga: Understanding the Gita and the Sutras*." He looked over at his writing partner. "Sucheta, would you please read the opening sentence from the manuscript?"

As always, it took Tiffany a few moments to respond to her Sanskrit name. When she realized that her guru was speaking to her, she reached for a stack of papers. "Of course Yogi. It says: Now begins the study of yoga."

"Now begins the study of yoga," Yogi Krishna Soham echoed. "Do you know where that sentence comes from?"

"Isn't it the first yoga sutra by Patanjali?" Thomas responded.

"Excellent, mister Thomas. And what does that sentence mean?"

"That it is time to study yoga?"

"Yes, but it means more than that," Yogi Krishna retorted. "Think."

"I don't know," Thomas said. "Does it mean that the student must be ready to start learning yoga?"

"Yes. It means that the student must be ready," Yogi Krishna said and leaned forward. His eyes gleamed with excitement as he looked around the room. "And when is the student ready?" he asked the group.

His question was met with silence. The students looked around, searching for someone who might know the answer.

126

"When?" Yogi Krishna Soham repeated. "When is the student ready?"

"When worldly pursuits no longer excite," Sunita answered.

"Precisely, Sunita. Just like we spoke about in our private class this morning," Yogi Krishna Soham replied, giving his favorite devotee the nod. "A student of yoga must be fed up with worldly pursuits, understanding that such endeavors will eventually lead to pain. Chocolate may taste great for a moment, but eating chocolate for every meal will cause pain. Loving a person may result in temporary joy, but with deep attachment comes the possibility of great pain. Sexual intercourse may feel good in the short term, but continual grinding and giving free reign to wild passions will eventually lead to pain."

"Are you saying that the student of yoga should never allow for momentary pleasures because within each of those pleasures is also the seed of suffering?" Kurt asked, wanting to dissect the psychological aspect.

"No," Yogi Krishna Soham stated forcefully. "Of course, students of yoga can allow themselves momentary sensory pleasures, such as good food, pleasant aroma, and soothing music. However, the true student of yoga understands that he will not find what he is looking for by searching further in that direction. The senses pull his consciousness outwards. No, the true student of yoga understands that the quest for meaning and happiness is an inward journey."

"I'm sorry, Yogi Krishna," BJ responded, "but if that is the prerequisite, then I guess that none of us are ready to be real students of yoga. By what I gather, we are all pretty externally oriented in addition to wanting to find some inner peace."

"Ahh, my Icelandic friend, but, in your case, seeds have been sown. You are still here. You know there is truth to what I am saying. You already sense that by changing direction in your pursuit of happiness, you might actually find something of great worth. At the same time, I am aware that yours will remain a part-time pursuit for now." Yogi Krishna Soham turned to Thomas and asked him directly: "You recognized the first yoga sutra, mister Thomas, but do you know who the sutras were created for?"

"For yoga students?" Thomas replied tentatively.

"In a manner of speaking, yes. The sutras were created for forest- and cave dwellers, the secluded pursuers of spirit who had abandoned the world in search of internal bliss. The sutras were created as a guide for serious spiritual seekers and were passed from man to man until, finally, Yogi Patanjali wrote the sutras down."

"So, Patanjali didn't create the sutras?" Thomas asked. His bulging muscles were stretching the hemp fabric of the clothes he had bought for the graduation earlier in the day.

"No, mister Thomas. Patanjali only wrote them down. In so doing, he changed the way in which yoga was transmitted. Up until then, it had only been transmitted from master to student. The sutras had only been taught to those who had shown themselves worthy. Once the sutras were available in written format, that age old process changed."

"I know people in the yoga teacher community who earnestly try to live by the *Yoga Sutras*, but they have not abandoned the world," Valentina said, "nor do they have gurus. What would you say to that?"

"I would say they are deluded, miss Valentina," Yogi Krishna Soham replied. "Living by the *Yoga Sutras* is a full-time pursuit. We can indeed extract wisdom from the sutras and apply it to our daily lives, but anyone who is still engaged in worldly pursuits and pretends to live by the sutras lacks the basic understanding needed to even begin the journey. Those people haven't even reached the first sutra, the point of being ready. They most likely apply the yogic disciplines in a mechanical and external way without understanding the essential first step, which is choosing a direction. The choice is between the world, on one hand, and that which does not change on the other. One path leads to attachment and pain. The other leads to freedom and bliss."

"You say we can extract wisdom from the *Yoga Sutras*, but not live by them. What is the difference?" Edna asked, sitting in the middle of the room. She took a sip of her tea.

"Listen to these words again, miss Edna. Now begins the study of yoga. The sentence implies two things. One, that the student has had enough of the world, and two, that he has chosen a direction, decided to move inwardly in search of peace and bliss. In a world where everyone is obsessed with outward appearance, it is easy to miss the internal direction and instead focus on the many external physical practices offered by the compilation of verses Patanjali assembled. I tell you that you are better off knowing nothing of the practices and embracing the direction than you are if you embrace every single one of the practices and miss the direction."

"So, if I understand you correctly," Laurie looked up from her notebook and summarized, "you are saying that even if we can't live by the sutras, we can be inspired by them."

"Precisely, miss Laurie. We can be inspired by them. Finding inspiration should be your focus in this advanced teacher training. Even if you don't join a monastery or move into a cave, you can be inspired by the direction chosen by yogis and yoginis throughout the ages, be inspired by the inward journey."

Yogi Krishna Soham smiled as he looked at the people in the room.

"Now begins the study of yoga," he said. "Say it with me."

"Now begins the study of yoga," they said in harmony.

Chapter Nineteen

The first week of the advanced portion of the yoga teacher training went by fast. The lectures were engaging — a combination of philosophy, teaching techniques, teacher etiquette, and marketing — and the yoga classes were more challenging than during the first two hundred hours, both because Yogi Krishna Soham taught at a higher level and because the teacher trainees were trying out new teaching methods in the afternoon classes.

Tiffany, who Yogi Krishna insisted on calling Sucheta, was at the ashram every day, working on their new writing project, and was becoming fast friends with Edna.

On the flip side, Valentina went out of her way to avoid contact with BJ after their healing session the previous Saturday night. He felt bad for having let his romantic feelings shine through. They weren't there anymore — had simply been a momentary lapse — but he didn't care to explain that to her. Things would even out eventually. If they didn't, it really wouldn't matter as they only had two weeks left of the yoga teacher training.

BJ noticed that Govinda became increasingly sullen as the week wore on and tried to leverage their newfound camaraderie to ask him why, but Govinda rejected any such attempts. He was friendly enough, but nowhere near confiding in BJ.

Having kept Camille's insinuations to himself, BJ couldn't help but carefully monitor the interactions between Tiffany and Yogi Krishna Soham. Try as he might, he noticed nothing improper or sexual in their behavior towards each other. Their relationship seemed to be professional in every way. If anything, BJ could not figure out why Tiffany was there in the first place. She looked out of place. She belonged in a university setting, not at an ashram.

"Today, we cleanse," Yogi Krishna Soham stated to everyone's surprise after exercises on Friday morning. He went on to explain that the students would be divided into two groups after morning class and, instead of eating breakfast, they would engage in a number of cleansing techniques found in the *Yoga Sutras* and *Hatha Yoga Pradipika*. The men were to go with Yogi Krishna Soham, while Rukmini — who the women secretly hated — was to lead the women in their cleansing efforts. Lilavati would assist both groups.

"Why divide the group by sex?" Laurie asked as they got ready to go outside. "Isn't that kind of sexist?"

"Trust me," Govinda responded with a smile, "you don't want to see us do this, nor would you want us to see you. Plus, we need to partially undress so as not to damage our clothes."

His explanation seemed to placate her.

Once outside, Thomas, BJ, Govinda, Kurt, and Yogi Krishna Soham gathered around a large steel pot filled with warm salt water. Yogi Krishna and Govinda took off their shirts, and the other three men followed suit.

"So, what are we doing exactly?" BJ asked, wary of what was about to happen. He had never participated in a cleansing of any kind in his life.

"First, we drink as much of this warm salt water as we possibly can," Yogi Krishna explained.

Without further instructions, he picked up a plastic cup, dipped it into the steel pot, and guzzled down a full glass in one sip.

"Come on," he said, "start drinking."

The saltwater tasted vile, and BJ had difficulty downing the first glass. When he dipped the cup in for a second time, Govinda, Thomas, and Yogi Krishna were already on their fourth glass. Kurt was on his third. BJ felt like he was losing a contest and had no idea what they were going to do next, but he kept on drinking, glass after glass. Yogi Krishna stopped after downing a little over nine cups. BJ felt full after three but pushed himself to swallow four and a half cups in total.

"Good," Yogi Krishna Soham said. "Now we churn."

He leaned forward, bent his legs, grabbed his thighs just above the knees, straightened his arms, emptied his lungs and pulled his bellybutton in towards his spine. It looked like his abdominal area all but disappeared. His ribcage was clearly visible, and his midsection was down to four or five inches in thickness. Then he let out his central abdominal muscles and started churning them from side to side, creating what seemed to be a circular movement to the untrained eye. After almost a minute of this, Yogi Krishna Soham stood up and inhaled.

Govinda followed suit and replicated his master's movements perfectly, but try as they might, the other three men could not do the same. At most, they were able to produce an in and out movement with their abdomen, but not the circular churning movement. Yogi Krishna did a few additional rounds himself, encouraging the other men in between.

When he was satisfied that enough churning had been done, Yogi Krishna declared: "Now, we eliminate."

"What?" BJ managed to exclaim despite the discomfort that had been caused by the saltwater and attempts at churning.

Yogi Krishna Soham and Govinda didn't explain, rather they thrust two fingers down the back of their throats. Within seconds, the salt water came gushing out of their mouths and onto the grass.

"You want us to throw up?"

BJ was beside himself. He had never been able to throw up voluntarily, even when he was drunk, even when he knew that doing so would make him feel better.

Govinda looked up, eyes red, mucus infused spit dripping from his lips.

"Yes," he said, "throw up. Otherwise, you will feel like crap for the rest of the day."

BJ looked on as the four men pushed their fingers deeper down their throats. Kurt had the strongest reaction. His gushes spewed so powerfully out of his mouth that they traveled several feet in the air before they splashed on the ground. Because the men had not eaten that morning, the vomit was mostly mucus infused water, but it did contain slight bits of dissolved food from the day before.

The men grunted and groaned as they induced one gag reflex after another. BJ could hear a combination of grunting and screaming coming from the other side of the house. He could only imagine what some of the women were going through if Rukmini had given such minimalist instructions as Yogi Krishna had.

"Keep doing it until you get it all out," Yogi Krishna Soham said with spit dripping from his long beard.

"Come on, BJ," Kurt said. "Do it!"

Feeling as horrible as he did, BJ couldn't imagine that throwing up could make it worse. He was wrong. As he stuck his fingers down his throat, he gagged immediately, but nothing came out. His head was pounding, his heart racing.

"Push the fingers deeper," Govinda said.

BJ was now the center of attention as the other men had already finished their elimination process.

"Trust me, you'll feel a lot better once you are done," Thomas added.

BJ pushed his fingers deeper. Again, he felt a gag reflex, but only a few drops of water spilled out.

"Again!" Govinda urged him on.

Finally, on his third try, BJ felt as if a dam had broken. The water gushed out of his mouth with the force of a tidal wave. Some of it even came out through his nose. He coughed and grunted as his stomach cramped.

"Do it again!" Yogi Krishna Soham instructed.

Not believing that he was willfully doing this to himself, BJ kept going, creating one gush after another until all that was left were stomach cramps. When he stood up, he was teary eyed, and the bottom half of his face was covered in mucus infused saltwater. Yogi Krishna handed him a rag and told him to clean up.

"Feel better?" he asked.

"Yeah, I guess," BJ replied as he shook his head and wiped his face. He could still hear groaning and screaming noises coming from the other side of the house.

"Good. Once you train the stomach, the cleansing becomes easier."

BJ didn't know how to react. He couldn't imagine going through this ever again, not voluntarily anyway.

"Now, we clean the nasal passage."

Neti pots were handed out to each of the men, small containers that looked like watering cans with little spouts on the end. Yogi Krishna Soham dipped his pot into the salt water container, pulled it out once it was full to the brim, leaned his head to the left, stuck the spout into his right nostril and poured. Almost immediately, water started running out of his left nostril. When he had emptied the pot, he stood up and performed several breathing techniques, much like he was blowing his nose. Along with the rest of the water, small amounts of clear snot came out of his nose. He then repeated this process for the other side, leaning his head to the right and pouring salt water through his left nostril.

In comparison with the stomach elimination, BJ found the nasal cleansing easy. The sensation was foreign, a little ticklish, to be exact, but because the water did not run into the back of his throat, it was not as unpleasant as accidently sucking water in through the nose while swimming, which was the sensation that he had expected.

Once the five men had completed the cleansing process with the Neti pot, Lilavati brought out ten plastic catheter tubes and handed two to each of them.

"This one is a little tricky," Yogi Krishna Soham said. "It is meant to clean the passage between the nose and the back of the throat."

In line with his method of teaching, Yogi Krishna Soham did not offer any instructions, rather led by example. He stuck the thin end of the catheter into his left nostril, maneuvering it deeper and deeper until he could reach in through his mouth and pull it out. The catheter now stuck out through both his nose and mouth. He then used both hands to rub the catheter back and forth, like he was drying his back with a towel. Finally, he pulled the catheter out through his nose, threw it away, and used a clean one to do the same for the other nostril.

Thomas and Govinda followed suit, but BJ and Kurt struggled. Try as he might, BJ could not push the catheter further than one or two inches up his nose. As soon as he felt like it was going into his mouth cavity, a gagging reflex caused him to pull it out.

"Sorry, I can't do it," he finally said.

"Neither can I," Kurt agreed.

"That's fine," Yogi Krishna Soham said. "Now, for the final cleansing technique either Lilavati or myself can help you administer a salt water enema to cleanse your colon."

"I am sorry," BJ said, "I should know this word, but sometimes my English fails me. What is an enema?"

When Kurt explained that an enema involved injecting water into the lower bowels by way of the anus, BJ decided to pass.

"That was disgusting," Andrea exclaimed when the group was back in the common area of the sleeping quarters. "Seeing that old lady vomit, eyes red, spit dripping down her chin, counting how many beans she had for dinner last night. Yuck!"

She quivered in disgust.

"Yeah," Laurie chimed in, "and she didn't even tell us what we were about to do."

"Neither did Yogi Krishna Soham," BJ responded. "I was completely taken off guard."

"It wasn't that bad," Valentina said.

"You don't think it was bad?" Andrea retorted. "I would have thought that you, of all people, would have been more squeamish."

"Why? Because I take care of myself? One of the reasons why I look good and feel good is because I take care of both my insides and outsides. Regular cleansing, similar to what we just did, has been a part of my routine for several years now."

"I've been doing the Neti pot, stomach cleansing, and occasional enema since I was here last year," Edna agreed.

"Why didn't you tell us what we were getting into?" Poppy said, apparently shocked by the whole thing. "I mean, I never thought that people would do anything like this to themselves voluntarily."

"It's an age old technique," Thomas interjected. "There are cleansing and fasting ceremonies found in every spiritual tradition. There are significant health benefits, plus, it removes lethargy and improves meditation, making it easier to uncover that which does not change."

"I have to admit that I feel lighter, my head clearer," BJ confessed.

"You can try to glamorize it all you want, but I am never doing any of that again," Andrea declared.

"I have to ask," BJ said, "Valentina, Thomas, do either of you ever teach these cleansing techniques to your yoga students?"

"I've never done it," Thomas replied.

"Neither have I, not yet anyway," Valentina concurred.

"Would you ever?" BJ asked.

"I don't know."

"It wouldn't be wise," Kurt said from where he stood, leaning up against the wall, "not in our society. In my line of work, I see excessive cleansing go hand in hand with disorders, such as anorexia and bulimia nervosa. Having seen the devastating and often life-threatening effects firsthand, I would advise against legitimizing such inclinations by introducing extreme cleansing techniques, like the ones we just engaged in. In my mind, yogic cleansing should never go mainstream."

Chapter Twenty

"BJ! Wait up!" Andrea quickened her step to get alongside BJ. They were on their way from the sleeping quarters to the yoga hall on a Saturday night to listen to Yogi Krishna Soham's evening lecture.

"I really enjoyed your class this afternoon," she said.

"Thanks," BJ replied, "at least I didn't freeze this time around."

"No, I mean it. You have talent. The class was to the point, and no energy was wasted on superfluous directions. It reminded me a little of Yogi Krishna."

"Thanks, I guess."

"It's a compliment mister I-hide-all-my-feelings. Take it."

"Okay then. Thank you."

"How's your dad doing?"

BJ stopped to take off his shoes in front of the main entrance.

"He's doing better. They say he can go home this week."

"That's excellent news."

"Yeah, quite a relief."

Andrea tugged on BJ's elbow when he was about to enter the building.

"Come over here for a moment. I have some news."

"News or gossip?"

"Don't be such an ass. Come here."

They stepped to the side of the entrance, allowing the other students to get in. It was already dark, and a choir of chirping crickets provided sound cover for Andrea.

"Did you hear about what happened today during lunch break?"

"No, what happened," BJ asked nonchalantly.

"Poppy overheard Lilavati scolding Yogi Krishna Soham, screaming at him in the kitchen."

"What was she saying?"

"See. I knew you would be interested," Andrea said with a sly smile as she poked BJ in the belly. "Poppy doesn't understand Hindi, or whatever language they speak to each other, but she was definitely scolding him. Her voice was thunderous and, according to Poppy, Yogi Krishna looked like he was cowering, unlike his confident, bordering on arrogant self."

"So? They fight. They've been married for decades. What's the big deal?"

"The big deal? She's not his servant, that's what. She has much more control over him than any of us can imagine. And she has a temper. He may look like the master, but, if what Poppy said is true, and I have no reason to doubt her, then we have completely misjudged the dynamics in their relationship."

"You mean that you've misjudged the relationship. I haven't thought much about it at all."

"Oh, come on mister high-and-mighty. You're not above the gossip. I know that you guys talk about the dynamics between Yogi Krishna and Govinda all the time. This is just the same, even more important if you think about how many women study yoga. It shows that Yogi Krishna Soham is not the dominant patriarch he appears to be, at least, not on all levels."

"We've talked about the culture differences, and I see your point, but what we're doing is still not gossip."

"Argh! You can be so infuriating."

"Then stop feeding me gossip," BJ said with a smile. "Come on. We'll be late for the lecture."

Once inside, BJ and Andrea joined the six other students, plus Lilavati, Govinda, Sunita—who had just finished her private class with Yogi Krishna—doctor Jaipur Mehta, and Tiffany.

After chanting Aum together and sitting still for approximately five minutes, the group became transfixed on Yogi Krishna Soham as he delivered his talk on prana.

"As I have told you many times before," he said, "prana is not mystical. Prana is like electricity. Even if we don't see prana, it doesn't mean it's not there. We know that electricity is present because electronic devices work. We are aware that prana is present because we can sense the energy. Everyone knows instinctively if another person is high energy or low energy. It is not magic. It is a law of nature."

Yogi Krishna's hair was unusually unruly. On normal days he would wet his hands and tidy his hair and beard before lectures, but tonight he looked as if he had just gotten out of bed.

"If the yogi or yogini is to master control of life energy, then there needs to be understanding of the underlying principles, some of which I will talk about tonight. The energy channels, through which prana is said to flow, are called the nadis. There are said to be approximately seventy-two thousand nadis in the body, roughly similar to the nervous system. Of these, three are major channels, named Ida, Pingala, and Sushumna."

Following their regular pattern, students were writing furiously while the guests kept their eyes trained on Yogi Krishna Soham the entire time.

"Ida is the lunar or feminine energy channel. Pingala is the solar or masculine energy channel. Both curl around the spine like snakes. Linear to the spine lies the central energy channel, namely Sushumna. When balance is reached between Ida and Pingala, the Kundalini energy, also known as the serpent energy, is awakened. It shoots up Sushumna, causing each of the energy centers, or chakras, to awaken. When the Kundalini energy reaches the seventh chakra, the yogi or yogini becomes enlightened, experientially knowing the permanent existence of that which does not change."

Yogi Krishna Soham paused to allow for questions about how to spell the Sanskrit names, deferring to Govinda, who meticulously spelled out each word, his mood still noticeably sour.

"The awakening of Kundalini is no easy feat. It takes years of purification and practice. First, the practitioner's goal is to awaken prana, to allow prana to flow unrestricted through each and every one of the seventy-two thousand nadis. Second, the practitioner must balance the energy flowing through Ida and Pingala and purify the chakras. Third, the practitioner must be prepared, must be physically, emotionally, and mentally purified, to withstand the Kundalini awakening. If he or she is not ready, the awakening of Kundalini can cause irreparable damage to the nervous system, causing everything from paralysis to insanity."

All the students looked up.

"Is it safe to practice then?" asked Edna.

"The answer to that question is both yes and no, miss Edna. A person who seeks to awaken Kundalini must practice fastidiously under the guidance of a guru. Cleansing, such as the one we engaged in yesterday, is an indispensable part of the process, but so is mental and emotional cleanliness, hence the yamas and niyamas. Practicing without guidance and without purification can be extremely dangerous."

"Have you awakened Kundalini?" Laurie asked forthrightly.

Yogi Krishna Soham burst into laughter.

"Have I?" he repeated. "Allow me to demonstrate."

He stood up, walked to the middle of the yoga hall, rolled out a mat, and said: "Gather around."

The group created a circle around the mat and sat down.

Standing on the mat, Yogi Krishna Soham took off his long sleeve hemp shirt and removed his mala beads. Dressed only in his off-white hemp pants and a white tank top, the old man began moving through a series of standing exercises with his eyes closed, using ujjayi breathing in rhythm with every movement. To BJ he sounded like Darth Vader from *Star Wars*. Within two or three minutes it was evident that his body temperature had risen considerably. Perspiration stained both the front and back of his tank top, pearls were beading on his forehead.

Having performed the exercises for about five minutes, he sat down, assumed the lotus pose in two swift yet graceful movements, straightened his back completely, and began vigorously breathing like he was blowing his nose rhythmically. Each exhalation was more forceful than the one before. After fifty or sixty rounds of that, Yogi Krishna exhaled, emptied his lungs, straightened his arms, curled his fingers, pulled his belly button in, and created an almost perfect ninety-degree angle at his neck by bringing his chin to his chest. Holding that position, the guru shook visibly. After two minutes, he raised his head, which created a straight line from his tailbone to his crown, and repeated the vigorous breathing exercise. When he exhaled again and brought his chin to his chest, the group of onlookers held their breaths.

He shook.

He trembled.

Then, with an audible popping sound and no visible muscle movement, Yogi Krishna Soham's body jumped five inches off the floor. The spectacle elicited audible gasps.

Once more, his head returned to an upright position, and he repeated the breathing technique, this time with astounding force. Again, with his feet still bound in lotus pose his chin returned to his chest. The spectators were leaning forward. Most of them looked like they didn't believe their own eyes. Even Govinda had his mouth open. Only Lilavati held her stoic calm.

Again, he shook, he trembled.

The second popping sound was louder, and again, with no visible muscle movement, Yogi Krishna Soham's body jumped, this time almost fifteen inches of the floor.

The group responded in awe.

"Wow."

"No way."

"Whaaat?"

"Unbelievable."

Lilavati put her index finger to her lips, and her tiny gesture silenced the group immediately.

Yogi Krishna Soham raised his head once again and deliberately slowed down his breathing. His body came to a standstill. There was absolutely no visible movement. It didn't even look like he was breathing. The energy in the room became peaceful beyond belief. Many of the students closed their eyes, savoring the peaceful energy, but BJ's eyes were glued on Yogi Krishna Soham. What on earth was he witnessing?

Finally, Yogi Krishna resumed rhythmic breathing, and his body began to show signs of life. When he opened his eyes, the room burst into spontaneous applause. The whites in Yogi Krishna's eyes shone like they had just been waxed and polished. He motioned for the applause to stop, then stood up, put on his shirt and mala beads, and found his way back to the stage while Govinda rolled up his mat. His skin was glistening as he sat down on the stage. The group moved towards him again. This time, everyone was drawn closer, huddled in together.

"That," Yogi Krishna Soham finally said after gently massaging his face and hands, "was a small taste of the Kundalini energy."

"How did you do that?" Poppy exclaimed, echoing the disbelief felt by her fellow students.

"Knowing how is only for the worthy, miss Poppy," he responded with a broad smile, seemingly radiating with energy, "and I am afraid that none of you are worthy, yet. However, now you know that Kundalini exists, just like you know that electricity exists when you see an electronic device at work."

"I don't understand," BJ said, sounding confused, "what is this Kundalini energy?"

"Hah!" Yogi Krishna Soham responded. "What is Kundalini? It is so obvious. It is the serpent energy. Virgin Mary is always depicted standing on a snake because she mastered the serpent energy, she had risen above it."

"I still don't understand," BJ replied.

"It is in the name, mister BJ," Yogi Krishna Soham said as if it were obvious. "Kundalini. Kunda. Sound it out. Kunda. It means cunt. Kundalini is the sexual energy!"

Chapter Twenty-One

"I can't believe he said that," Valentina cried when the students had gathered in the common area back in the sleeping quarters. The women were clearly upset, outraged.

"I know," Andrea chimed in, "what a chauvinist."

"Sexist pig," Laurie piled on.

BJ couldn't tell whether or not she was joking.

"Did I miss something?" BJ said. "Why are all of you so upset?"

"Didn't you hear what he said, BJ?" Valentina responded angrily.

"Sure, I heard everything he said, but maybe I missed something. I was still in awe of his demonstration," BJ replied in earnest. "Did you see how he popped off the floor? I am still trying to wrap my head around that. I don't understand exactly why you are acting this way. Even if I may regret it, I'll ask again. What made you so upset?"

"The c-word," Valentina replied in dismay. "Nobody uses that unless he or she, usually he, intends to seriously degrade women?"

"I am sorry, the c-word —"

"Don't be so daft, BJ," Edna said, adding her voice to the mix. "Yogi Krishna said cunt, alright, cunt, and for most women, that's not okay."

"Really?" BJ said. He was truly astonished. "After everything that happened tonight, that's your takeaway? He said the word cunt? I don't get it."

"It is the most offensive word a man can use," Valentina replied.

"But it's only a word," BJ responded. "People use English curse words all the time in Iceland, including fuck, shit, cunt, dick, and probably worse. In fact, many people back home think that all Americans talk like that."

"Well, here such words are taken seriously, BJ," Poppy said, almost like she was scolding him.

"I still don't get it," BJ scoffed, "are all of you this offended because he said that one word? It wasn't like he was saying it about you. He was explaining a concept. Kunda is cunt. It's eerie because in Icelandic the same word is kunta. I get it. That's why he doesn't have sex, to maximize his Kundalini energy. Back me up here guys."

"I don't know," Thomas said reluctantly, "the c-word is pretty offensive."

"Yeah, but he did not say it about the women, did he," BJ replied. "What do you think, Kurt?"

Kurt leaned back and crossed his arms.

"I think…"

"Yes."

"I think that we should try to overlook his use of the c-word. As BJ pointed out, it was a direct translation of the first half of the word Kundalini. Plus, it may serve us well to remember the old saying: Sticks and stones may break my bones, but words can never hurt me."

"Is that your opinion as a psychologist," Andrea said in a hostile tone.

"Yes, I think that Yogi Krishna Soham meant no offense."

"Then you are an idiot," Andrea chided him. "Yogi Krishna has lived in this country long enough, been around enough women, to know that the c-word is offensive, no matter the context. Furthermore, words can cause emotional harm. You of all people should know that."

"Come now, Andrea. Don't be so bitchy," BJ said. "You didn't need to call him an idiot."

"Now you've done it," Thomas said, "I'm outta here."

He stood up and marched into his room.

Andrea gave BJ what could only be described as a death stare.

"Oh, it's okay for you to call my friend Kurt here an idiot, but when I describe your behavior as bitchy, then I am going too far? It seems to me that there is a double standard when it comes to communications here. Women are allowed to be super sensitive on the one end and then say whatever they want on the other."

"Asshole—" Andrea retorted.

"Let's all take a deep breath now," Kurt said.

"Yeah," Edna agreed, "let's not start a full blown gender war."

"No, let's," Laurie said with glee. "I am in dire need of some entertainment."

"Is this all a joke to you? Weren't you offended by what Yogi Krishna said, Laurie?" BJ asked, turning his attention to her.

"Not really," she replied, "like Kurt said, I try not to take words too seriously, plus, me and my friends use that word all the time when we are joking around."

"And you, Edna?"

"I was a little offended, but I'll get over it."

"So, it was mainly Valentina and Andrea who took offense," BJ concluded. "Why?"

"Because," Valentina replied hastily, "the c-word is deeply misogynistic, and it has no place in a yoga teacher training."

"Even if it is the direct translation of Kunda?"

"Even if," she said.

"And you agree, Andrea?"

"Yeah, I think he went too far this time."

"Okay then," BJ replied, wanting to back off and make peace. "I don't get it, but if it is important to the two of you I won't question your indignation any further—and Andrea, I apologize for implying you were a bitch."

"Apology accepted—asshole," she replied with a sly smile. It was evident that the wound wasn't very deep.

"You want to talk about it some more, Valentina," BJ continued, trying to soften things up.

"No, I'm okay," she responded. "I guess you were right. He didn't direct his words to us personally. Maybe I did overreact a little."

"You guys are no fun," Laurie said in her signature playful voice. "I'm going to bed."

"Good night, Laurie," they all said as she went to her room.

BJ took a deep breath that soon turned into a yawn. Within a minute, everyone in the room was yawning as well.

"I know we are all tired," BJ said, shaking off the yawn, "but can we please talk a little bit about what happened tonight, not the c-word, but the Kundalini display that Yogi Krishna Soham put on for us. Am I the only one who was blown away by that?"

"No," Kurt said, leaning forward, "I am still having a hard time processing what I just saw. Was it a display of something real or did Yogi Krishna just perform a very realistic magic trick."

"That's the very definition of magic, isn't it," Edna said, "that it must defy our version of reality and look realistic."

"You think it was real, Edna?" BJ asked.

"I don't know," she replied. "From my work as a lawyer, I know all too well that the brain can deceive. Witness testimony, for example, is notoriously unreliable. However, I trust Yogi Krishna, even though I may not always agree with him wholeheartedly. I don't know why he would trick us into believing something like that."

"So you think it was real?" Kurt followed up.

"Until proven otherwise, yes," Edna replied. "Fantastical. Mystical. But real."

"What about you, Poppy?" BJ asked, turning towards the aerobics teacher who sat huddled in the corner in her off-white hemp clothes. Aside from the twice-daily yoga classes, she seemed to have discarded her activewear entirely for the modest hemp clothes after the second part of the teacher training began.

"I don't know what to believe," she said resignedly, out of character.

"I think that what happened is as real as anything," Kurt offered. "Granted that reality often depends on our perception, but, like it or not, we had a communal perception earlier tonight that we cannot explain other than by accepting what we saw. How he did it, I don't know, but he did it."

"What does that mean?" BJ asked out loud, as much of himself as of the others.

"As much as I hate to admit it," Kurt mused, "I think it means that this no sex thing works."

"That's what I am beginning to think as well," BJ agreed.

Chapter Twenty-Two

The following Sunday began typically enough. At six in the morning, Yogi Krishna Soham led the group through breathing techniques, mantra chanting, and meditation. At seven, Poppy taught the asana class and got everyone sweating and panting with her version of yoga — which could only be described as aerobics or rajas yoga — and then Govinda taught hands-on adjustments.

When the clock struck eleven that morning, ushering in the day's seva, or service hour, everything began to unravel. In fact, people started to act so erratically that, even though BJ did not believe in its power to stir emotions, he was tempted to look at the moon that night to see whether or not it was full.

To begin with, Govinda worked as if he were possessed during seva. Instead of their usual ten trees an hour quota, Thomas, BJ, Kurt and Govinda planted sixteen trees within that timeframe. The intense heat had everyone sweating bullets.

"What's gotten into him?" Kurt asked BJ. "He might as well have a whip on us the way he is acting now. Hasn't he ever heard of taking it easy on Sundays?"

"I don't know," Thomas replied and wiped his brow. His broad shoulders were darkly tanned, and the tan further defined his muscles, which had shrunk a little during his time at the ashram because he had not gotten a chance to lift weights like he normally did.

"I think it has something to do with Lulu," BJ suggested.

"Lulu? Are the two of them a couple?" Kurt asked.

"Sort of," BJ replied, "at least, that is what I think. I shouldn't be gossiping, but Govinda's mood seems to have gotten grouchier with each passing day that she hasn't shown up at the ashram."

"I hope she comes back soon or that he gets over it," Kurt said while panting. "I won't be able to take many days like this."

"Back to work guys!" Govinda shouted as he wheeled in a fresh pile of manure.

After seva, BJ took his usual walk down to the strip mall to call Sara. On his way back, he saw Poppy across the street, running as fast as he'd ever seen her run. He tried to call out, but she seemed locked in. From a distance, it looked like she had been crying.

Walking into the sleeping quarters, BJ saw Thomas sitting behind Laurie, massaging her shoulders. She had her top off, covering her breasts with only a towel. BJ didn't say anything, rather went straight to his room.

"That boy is playing with fire," BJ said to Kurt while he was changing from his sweat-drenched clothes.

"Why do you say that?" Kurt replied.

"Because, if Laurie has shown us anything, it is that she is a very sexual young lady. She doesn't hide it when she's horny, even brags about sleeping with the next available person, be it a man or woman. Even if Thomas thinks he is just giving her a massage, he is opening a door. I hope he realizes that."

"What an excellent diagnosis," Kurt mocked. "Did you buy a psychology degree at the strip mall?"

"Come on. It doesn't take a psychology degree to see what can happen in close quarters like this."

"That might be," Kurt replied, "but it's not our place to judge. They are grown ups. They have to decide what they want for themselves."

"True, but I just don't want to see Thomas — who speaks with such affection about his wife and little kid — ruin his future prospects unknowingly. I don't think he knows what he is doing."

"And you think we should talk to him?"

"Couldn't hurt, could it?" BJ said and shrugged his shoulders. "We'll just ask him if he's thought this thing through."

"He'll tell us that it was a harmless shoulder massage and that there's nothing to worry about."

"Yes, but the thought will be in his mind. He might be more

careful for the remainder of our time here."

"Okay," Kurt said, as both of them got ready to leave the room. "We'll talk to him tonight."

On their way to class, Kurt and BJ passed Edna's room. She was sitting next to Tiffany and was evidently upset.

"He doesn't deserve you," Tiffany was saying, "you are so much better than that—"

Upon seeing them, Tiffany stood up and closed the door.

"What do you think that was about?" BJ asked as they stepped out and slipped on their flip-flops. The two o'clock thunderstorm was already under way.

"You were such a level-headed guy when you arrived here," Kurt said. "I think Andrea's constant gossiping is getting to you. Just let it go. It's not our concern."

"You're right," BJ said sheepishly and ran under the walkway, water splashing on his bare toes.

The second lecture of the day was uneventful and so was dinner, but when Andrea and BJ made their way from the sleeping quarters to the yoga hall that night for the weekly Sunday evening Satsang, they were stopped by Rukmini.

"Why do you not bow to Gurudev during Satsang?" she demanded.

"That's none of your business," Andrea replied.

"It is," Rukmini said in a haughty tone. "Gurudev is an inspired spiritual being. Every day he pours from his cauldron of wisdom in your presence, and you don't have the humility to realize that. The least you can do is bow to him once a week."

"We paid for this program," Andrea countered, "there is no need to bow just because everyone else is doing it."

"You misunderstand," Rukmini said in response. "The bowing is for you, not for him. You are reminding yourself that you are in the presence of an enlightened master. You are opening your containers for his wisdom. You are making yourselves into spiritual vessels."

"Yeah," BJ interjected, "thanks for the advice Patricia, but I am just not the bowing kind."

"You will address me with the name that Yogi Krishna has bestowed upon me, as Rukmini, the namesake of the first wife of Lord Krishna."

BJ was taken aback by her directness. She sounded like an aristocrat scolding one of her servants.

"Of course," he said, not wanting to instigate an argument that he knew could win intellectually, but wasn't so sure he could defend emotionally. "Rukmini it is. Shall we step inside? The Satsang is about to begin."

At Satsang, the questions were mostly about teaching poses and interacting with students. As usually, Yogi Krishna Soham did a good job of answering directly, and it seemed as though the women had gotten over the c-word remark, at least they didn't show any outward behavior to suggest they were offended.

Returning to the sleeping quarters, BJ once again walked alongside Andrea. Although he wasn't into her gossip, he liked her directness. She reminded him of several Icelandic women that he knew, the ones who spoke directly and were mostly free from drama. Admittedly, he also felt comfortable in her presence because he felt no sexual attraction towards her.

The clouds had cleared, and the stars were shining brightly. BJ was unused to the combination of balmy temperatures and starry skies. Summer nights in Iceland were bright so that there were never any stars visible. Looking up, he noticed that the moon was full after all. Hopefully, the dramatics of the day were over.

"Did you see how Sunita was holding her belly during Satsang?" Andrea asked.

"No," BJ replied, "I can't say that I did."

"I think she is pregnant," Andrea continued.

"Come on Andrea," BJ said as he slipped off his shoes and placed them on the shoe rack outside the sleeping quarters, "Kurt said today that your gossiping was rubbing off on me. Can't you just observe what is going on around you without making up stories?"

"I am telling you," she continued, oblivious to his comments. "I've seen women cup their belly's with two hands like that before and every time, every time I tell you, they have been pregnant."

BJ shook his head.

"Even if she is," he said, "it's none of our business."

"Wouldn't it be interesting, though," Andrea kept on imagining, "I mean, she isn't married and has never mentioned that she is in a relationship. Who could the father be?"

"I am not doing this with you," BJ said with a smile, shook his head and entered the building. "Good night, Andrea."

After the three roommates had finished their traditional philosophical dialogue — including a mention of Thomas's massage tactics with Laurie, which he, foreseeably, shrugged off — the lights were turned off. The full moon day had come to an end, or so BJ thought, until screaming from the foyer awoke him.

"Come out here, quickly," a female voice cried.

BJ, Thomas, and Kurt, all rushed out into the common area, where the women had already gathered. Govinda came running down the stairs.

"What is it?" he said sternly.

"It's Edna," Poppy replied, looking visibly shaken where she sat next to Edna who was lying on the floor, crying and writhing. "She went out for an evening run and lay down in the fields behind the ashram to admire the moon. She landed directly on top of a fire ant farm. She is covered in ant bites."

"I'll get the car," Govinda said in haste. "We are taking her to the hospital."

Chapter Twenty-Three

At two o'clock on Wednesday afternoon, the group sat in the yoga hall faced with a spritely sixty-seven-year-old Indian gentleman. His name was Gadin Dhaduk, Yogi Krishna's older brother. He was thin but muscular, cleanly shaven, with short trimmed gray hair, dressed in beige khaki shorts, a dark blue, short sleeved, silk shirt, wearing a gold Rolex watch on his wrist, and a gold chain around his neck. He bounced onto the stage and sat down in a perfect lotus pose.

Govinda had prepped the group for the older brother's arrival, but none of the year-round residents were on the premises when he arrived. BJ wondered why.

Only seven students were in the room with the guest teacher, as Edna was still recovering from the fire ant bites. She'd gotten a shot at the hospital on Sunday night and been prescribed rest and plenty of anti-itch cream. Predictably, Andrea had gotten the scoop. Edna had been upset because her husband had confessed and told her that he'd cheated on her while she was away. She had gone for a run that night to clear her head. Lying down in the grass in the darkness had been her cardinal mistake.

With the watchful eyes of Krishna surrounding them in his many depictions on the walls, the group gathered close to the stage, eager to learn what the older brother of their yoga master had to offer.

"Hello," he said, followed with a warm belly laugh. "I am Gadin Dhaduk."

The students couldn't help but smile and responded with hellos of their own.

"I don't know why he keeps inviting me," Gadin said, "I am no guru. I am retired. I worked my entire adult life as an engineer, but Gopal insists. He wants you to know what spiritual life is like for someone who has chosen to live in the world, not outside of it, protected in an ashram."

He smiled broadly, took off his gold Rolex watch and put in on the stage next to him.

"I have two hours with you. Let's make the most of them, shall we."

His English was next to flawless. There was no trace of the distinct Indian accent that his brother, the venerable Yogi Krishna Soham, had.

"There are only two important questions when it comes to spiritual life in the modern world. Does this practice or idea help me unveil that which does not change or does it cover that which does not change? Those are the two questions. Does it help me see the unchanging reality or does it bind me to the ever-changing reality? Gopal has told you this, yes?"

The group nodded, mindful of the fact that Yogi Krishna's birth name was Gopal.

"Okay, then it is easy to discern between that which is not yoga and that which is. Yoga is everything that helps the practitioner unveil that which does not change, no matter what everyone else calls it. If it doesn't help me reveal Atman, then it is not yoga. You get it?"

Gadin was so relaxed, so at home on stage, that BJ could hardly believe that he wasn't a teacher.

"Gopal has spoken to you about the chakras, right, about the energy centers?"

"Yes," Valentina responded.

"What did you think?"

"That one needs to balance the energy centers in order find harmony," Valentina offered.

"Sure, that's one way to look at that philosophy. It's easy to see it as some sort of yoga psychology where a person has to find a balance between competing elements in the psyche, everything from physical security, to sexual energy, to self-identity, to emotional connection, to expression, intellect and so on. If that is how you see the chakras, then finding balance becomes a goal in itself, correct?"

"Correct," Valentina replied with a smile.

"I have chosen to see the chakras differently," Gadin said with levity. "To me, the chakras present an obstacle course."

The brothers were similar in many ways, but Gadin presented himself with a kind of nonchalant self-confidence that seemed to say: I couldn't care less about what you think of me.

"How so?" Kurt queried.

"If the goal is to unveil that which does not change," Gadin responded, "then every chakra presents a veil that keeps one from seeing the unchanging reality. Every chakra is an image that is cast upon the white screen of pure consciousness and keeps me from experiencing the whiteness of the screen."

The afternoon thunderstorm was brewing in the distance. The air conditioning unit was blowing cold. Govinda had said that Gadin didn't like to sweat. The cold air caused the women to drape their shoulders with blankets. Gadin stayed silent as he looked for recognition in the student's eyes.

"Ahh," he finally said. "Why do I even bother? You're not ready to hear this. You are all beginners, even if this is an advanced teacher training. You probably just want to ask me how many sun salutations I practice in the mornings."

"How many sun salutations do you practice?" Laurie asked in her signature playful tone.

"None. That's how many. I lift weights and run to maintain health. I only stretch enough to be able to sit still during meditation. See, this is what I mean. You people don't understand yoga. You think that poses are what yoga is, but the poses are only tools, only a means to an end. The real goal of yoga is to uncover that which does not change."

"I don't understand," Poppy responded. "You don't do any yoga positions, but you say you practice yoga. How can that be?"

"How long have you been here, miss?" Gadin responded. His tone was neither judgmental nor condescending. Rather, he sounded concerned.

"Almost four weeks now," she replied.

"And you are still asking this question? That is a problem."

"Why?"

"Because, it means that you don't truly understand."

"Look, we are here to become yoga teachers, not spiritual gurus," Andrea responded. "We've put up with all kinds of crap from your brother to be able to get our degree, but if you are not going to teach us then we don't need to deal with your patronizing attitude."

Gadin laughed warmly.

"Very direct," he replied. "I like that. What is your name?"

"Andrea."

"Well, Andrea, I am not trying to be an ass, although it may seem that way. I want to teach you, really, I do, but my teachings have to be built on some sort of foundation. I know that my brother has been trying to teach you real yoga, but there still seems to be a misunderstanding about what yoga really is."

"Why don't you enlighten us?" BJ interjected. "You can start by telling us what you mean by saying that the chakra system is like an obstacle course."

"Okay then," Gadin replied as if he'd just accepted a challenge. "As I said before, the chakras are obstacles because they veil that which does not change. In real yoga, the goal is to balance and maintain each one so it can be overcome. For example, the first chakra represents security — which mostly refers to money and health these days — so one spends an appropriate amount of time on health and income to be able to focus on unveiling that which does not change. The focus is on the word appropriate. I, for example, studied yoga postures when I was young, but after I had attained a certain degree of strength and flexibility, all I had to do was the minimum number of poses or movements to maintain what I had gained. Then I spent years learning to engineer, to make enough money so I didn't have to worry. Today, I have both enough money and good health. I obsess about neither one."

"So, that's it? Once you get it, you just stop?" Valentina asked.

"No, I maintain," Gadin replied with emphasis. "Let's take an example. When you learned how to read, you first had to learn the alphabet, correct?"

Everyone nodded.

"But once you'd learned the alphabet, you read to maintain it. You didn't have to go back to memorizing and learning each letter for hours every day, right?"

His question was met with several yesses, and that's rights.

"In the same way, why obsess over physical postures when one has reached the goal of finding a balance between strength and flexibility, and can sit for extended periods of time without experiencing any discomfort? What is the point in doing that?"

Most of the students shrugged their shoulders, but no one answered.

"I have met many self-reported yoga adherents who began their relationship with yoga by practicing postures for an hour every day. Now, fifteen years later, they are practicing yoga poses for two and a half to three hours a day. By focusing incessantly on the physical practice, they will eventually suffer because they will lose their health. It is the nature of the body. To me, that is wrong practice. They are investing their energy and time into something that will inevitably change. That is not yoga."

"How much is enough physical practice then?" Thomas asked.

"That depends, doesn't it? When one is starting out, the body needs attention. Pain is a dense veil. Until the body is balanced, one should practice for hours on end, but at some point, preferably when the body is mostly tension-free and able to sit for extended periods of time, the practice must evolve and go into maintenance mode."

"So, if yoga postures are good when a person is stiff and in pain, but not as important when balance has been achieved," Andrea said, lying on her abdomen like she did during most lectures, "then I'll probably be doing yoga postures for the rest of my life. I don't see this body attaining balance anytime soon."

"Does the same apply to the other chakras? Find balance and then maintain?" Kurt asked with interest.

"Yes," Gadin replied, showing the same characteristics that Yogi Krishna showed when one of his students appeared to comprehend what he was saying. "Balance them and maintain the balance for the purpose of unveiling that which does not change."

"I hear you saying that any practice we engage in can become a hindrance in itself."

It was the ant bitten lawyer, Edna. Her face was pale, and she moved gingerly as she sat down behind the other students.

"Edna, you should be in bed," Valentina said with worry in her voice.

"I am okay now, thank you. I took pretty strong painkillers an hour ago, and I wanted to see Yogi Krishna's older brother. It's an honor to meet you Mr. Dhaduk."

"Please, call me Gadin," he responded.

"Thank you, Gadin. My name is Edna."

"To answer your question, Edna, you are absolutely correct in saying that almost any practice can become a hindrance. Yogi Patanjali says in the Yoga Sutras that the yoga practitioner can fall in love with the toys he is presented with along the way and forget the end goal. Health can become a toy. Increased sexual energy can become a toy. A strong self-image can become a toy. Emotional sensitivity can become a toy. Effective communications can become a toy. Even the ability to focus intently can become a toy."

"Pretty powerful toys," Edna replied. "Easy to become addicted to using them."

"Yes, indeed," Gadin said with a broad smile. "Even meditation, if practiced incorrectly, can become a toy, veiling that which does not change."

"I still don't get it," Poppy cried. "Why unveil that which does not change? I'd love to have access to any one of those toys you just mentioned, better health, better sex, stronger self-image, better emotional life, more focus. If that's what yoga is about, deal me in, but that which does not change doesn't sound as appealing to me as the rest of it."

"What about unconditional love, happiness that does not depend on outside sources, perfect inner peace, and freedom from fear, even from the fear of death? Want those?"

"Sure," Poppy replied, raising her eyebrows.

"That which does not change is the source that provides all of those and more."

"Oh…"

"See, that is the ABC of yoga, the understanding that everything else is built on. Once you have that basic understanding, all you need is a direct experience to support the theory. That is where practice comes in."

"Why aren't you a teacher?" Poppy asked. "You seem to have the talent for it. At least you've helped me understand yoga a little better just now."

"When I was in my late teens, I had a direct personal experience of that which does not change," Gadin said, then paused like he was transporting himself back in time. "It was deep, powerful, and had lasting effects. I saw the building blocks of reality clearly. I saw the source from which everything flows. At that moment, I decided to build my life around maintaining that direct experience, remaining awake. For a while, I tried to be a teacher, but I got caught in it. I began to buy into all sorts of ideas about how yoga teachers should and should not act. I became too invested in the success or failure of my students. My guru, Swamidev, told me that I didn't have the personality to be a guru. He said that sometimes a guru needs to maintain the illusion for the benefit of the student and that I was too direct for that."

Gadin looked down to gather his thoughts, then turned halfway around in his seat, nodded to the picture of Swamidev hanging above his head and whispered something which none of the students could hear.

"He saved me," Gadin continued when he turned his attention

back to the students. "From that time on, I built my life around activities that could help me maintain my true identity, that allowed me to continue to unveil that which does not change. I learned how to do a job that required only my intellect and provided for a great retirement — a retirement that I am now enjoying. I married a woman who had similar inclinations and, although we are wealthy by modern standards, we have spent very little time gathering things around us. Together we have two children that I have cared for but have never tried to control. They have grown up to have the same interest in unveiling that which does not change."

"So, you don't want to be a guru, but were saved by a guru?" BJ asked.

"Guru is an interesting term. As you must know by now, the word guru means that which removes darkness or fog. Putting pictures of dead people up on walls, bowing to them, and telling everyone that they are your guru, all of that amounts to nothing. Only when someone sets you on a path, teaches you directly, challenges your assumptions about the world, and most importantly, leads you in the direction of that which does not change, does the term guru apply."

"You've certainly challenged our ideas," BJ replied, "even ideas that your brother has taught us."

"We have chosen different paths in life, my brother and I, but our goal is the same."

"Still, just in the hour and a half that you have been with us," BJ continued, "you have slaughtered some of the sacred cows that continually graze in this yoga hall. A part of me is better off from having heard you speak while another part of me is doubly confused. It makes me wonder why your brother wants you to teach here in the first place."

Gadin looked BJ directly in the eyes and replied: "Sometimes I wonder about that myself."

Chapter Twenty-Four

With a little over a week to go in the advanced yoga teacher training, BJ was feeling more confused than he'd been when he arrived. Although his body was feeling better than it had in years, his head was caught up in a whirlwind. On Thursday, the day after the older Dhaduk had graced them with his presence, BJ had spent his entire lunch break on the phone with Sara, telling her how he felt pulled in a thousand different directions.

"Why don't you write it all down?" she'd said.

"You mean, like in a diary?"

"Yeah, something like that. My friend, Drífa, read this book about emotions that was called *Slaying Your Dragons*. She said that the first step in the slaying process was to take the dragon's power away by reducing it from an out of control beast in the mind to a controllable creature on paper. Once out of the mind, the dragons appear smaller."

Slay dragons, huh?

After mulling the idea for a day — even talking briefly about it to his friend and resident psychologist Kurt, who said that if he was feeling confused, it probably wouldn't hurt — BJ decided to use the method and try to make some sense of his emotions.

As he walked purposefully towards the strip mall, his mind wandered back to the last time he wrote anything in a diary. It had been when he was twelve. Back then everyone was doing it, so he'd decided to give it a try. His mother had bought him a small leather-bound diary with a flimsy gold plated lock and a tiny key. He'd written about a girl he had a crush on, his first love, the golden-haired Brynhildur, who never loved him back. But after one of his friends had broken the lock and read out loud what he had written, BJ had never touched a diary again, never written about his thoughts or emotions, until now.

The strip mall was populated with a dry cleaner, an insurance office, a vapor store, a dollar store, a donut and coffee shop, and the Subway store BJ frequented. In the dollar store, BJ found a flimsy, ring-bound notebook with a blue cover and also bought a black ink pen.

Sitting in a corner booth inside the Subway store with a six-inch chicken teriyaki sub by his side, BJ opened the notebook, took out the black ink pen and wrote.

Dear diary…

He chuckled to himself, shook his head, crossed out the words, and ripped out the page. This would not be easy for him.

"If you don't know what to write," Sara's words from the day before echoed in his mind, "then write a question and attempt to answer it."

Why am I so confused?

After writing down the question, BJ took a large bite of his sub and looked out into the distance while he chewed. His gaze turned into a stare and the lunch traffic at Subway became a blur to him, the sounds became indecipherable. Then, suddenly, something in his mind clicked. He looked down and began writing like mad.

I am confused because I am being bombarded with inconsistent messages. Every day we spend hours on our bodies, stretching, strengthening, breathing, relaxing, cleansing, but then, during lectures, we are told that our bodies don't matter, that only 'that which does not change' matters.

I understand the idea, have even experienced some moments of peace during my stay here, but I can't see how it is relevant, not to the average yoga student or even to us, the so-called advanced yoga teacher trainees. We live in the world. We have to take care of our health, which is the main reason why

I began practicing yoga in the first place, in addition to wanting to please Sara. Plus, we need a way to reduce stress. Those two reasons for practicing yoga I understand, but the mantra chanting, philosophy, meditating, and the damn Krishna references, making the whole thing sound like religious festival...

I am confused because of all that. Because most of the people in the program, including me, need the services of a shrink more than they need far fetched philosophy about something which does not change.

After dad's bleeding ulcer, I have been consumed with ideas about my own mortality and of his impending death. I haven't spoken to anyone about that, not about death. What is there to say? While everyone else is preoccupied with sex and food, I am focused on death on the one hand and obsessed with health on the other.

Why am I even here?

I could have packed my bags after the two hundred hours and headed home. I didn't need more philosophy. I didn't need to attend yoga classes taught by my fellow students. Most of what we have been doing here for the past two weeks, I could have skipped or done on my own. I know more about marketing than the lot of them put together. Me and Sara, we have a good plan.

So, what have I gained from the advanced program?

More confusion, that's all.

Then there is Yogi Krishna. He is a mystery to me. He can reach deep states of meditation and pop off the floor with no apparent muscle movements, yet he can also be obnoxious, old-fashioned, right out misogynistic. One moment he is a sympathetic figure, the other he is like a dysfunctional father. He reminds me of why I don't like the Bible. Too many inconsistencies. Too many paradoxes.

And yet, I can't help but think that this is exactly what I needed, on some level. I have been so focused on making money and on following my penis that I have hardly stopped for a moment to feel or think, not for years. Maybe, just maybe, the confusion I am feeling these days is not all due to outside influences. Maybe, I am the source of the confusion. That would be an interesting discovery.

But, that's not all that is happening. No. There is some confusion on the inside, but the external paradoxes are too many to ignore.

What can I do?

I guess I'll just have to put my head down and power through this last week. Having the advanced degree, as Thomas has pointed out, makes me eligible to conduct a yoga teacher training of my own. That could be a boon for our yoga studio in Iceland. Could be worth this entire trip. Yes, I'll put my head down, stop thinking so much, and power through this last week. Then I'll make an appointment with a shrink when I get back home. Yeah, that sounds like a good plan.

BJ closed his notebook and looked up. To his amazement, he felt better. He hadn't resolved anything, not really, but that book Sara referenced had been right. Getting the turmoil out of his head and onto paper took away some of its power.

Smiling slightly, BJ finished his sub and walked back to the ashram in a calm and collected manner. One week was nothing. He would complete this program and then get back home to the love of his life. This would all be worth it. He would no longer allow the paradoxical Yogi Krishna to get under his skin.

"Did it work?" Kurt asked when BJ entered their sleeping quarters, ready for his midday change of clothes.

BJ looked up and smiled.

"I guess it did," Kurt responded. "Come on," he added, "we'll be late for Yogi Krishna's lecture on the *Bhagavad-Gita*."

Chapter Twenty-Five

"You look like a million bucks, my friend," Andrea said when BJ emerged from the massage room midday on Sunday.

The two of them stood together in the sleeping quarters hallway. Lulu was using the one remaining empty room for her massages.

"Yeah," BJ said with a smile, "I am happy that Lulu is back but also sad that she is going away again."

"She's going away?" Andrea responded.

"Yeah, she got a job offer that she can't refuse. She is moving to Vegas."

"To do what?"

"Don't know. Didn't ask. Just said I was happy for her."

"Have you learned nothing from our time together young padawan?" Andrea said, smiling broadly. "I only have six days left to ignite the curiosity spark that resides within you."

"Many have tried," BJ replied jokingly, "all have failed. I don't think I have it in me."

"I am not giving up," Andrea said, holding up her hands, Darth Vader style like she was trying to subdue him. "Come over to the dark side."

The two of them shared a laugh.

"Seriously, though," Andrea said, "I am going to miss you."

"Yeah, me too."

"How's your dad?"

"No news is good news. I am told that he is recovering, but we haven't spoken since he left the hospital. I am told that he is trying to hurry the process. He was never one to lie still for too long."

"Old school. I can respect that."

"Andrea," Lulu said, peeking out from behind the door. "I am ready for you now."

"Thanks," Andrea replied. "I'll see you when I get back from heaven, BJ."

"See you."

BJ walked out into the common area but found no one there. The time was only one o'clock, still an hour left before classes started again. He slipped on his flip-flops and ventured out into the field. The temperatures were abnormally low, in the high eighties or low nineties. BJ decided to take off his shirt while he strolled around the grounds. His friends back home wouldn't forgive him for having been in the sun for five weeks and not bringing home a tan. It was the Icelandic rule. When in the sun, bring back a tan.

Walking around leisurely, BJ marveled at all the gardening work that the group had done since he came to the ashram. Never before in his life had he planted a fruit tree, but now he could see the banana trees he'd planted in the first week starting to produce fruit. Some of the other fruit trees they'd planted had begun flowering as well. It was truly amazing, so unlike the slow pace of trying to grow anything in Iceland where one was lucky to receive a crop of potatoes and turnips once a year.

He picked a juicy passion fruit from an established tree and enjoyed taking small bites, savoring each one. The passion fruit was lunch. He'd skipped his usual trip to the strip mall, skipped his usual dose of meat for a massage. It had been worth it.

When BJ approached the far east end of the property, he came upon a huge black olive tree that produced plenty of shade. BJ felt that he could use a break from the sun and the leaf covered branches provided immediate relief. As he stood in the shade, taking deep breaths and stretching a little, BJ heard a sniffle.

"Is somebody there?" he called out.

"Leave me alone," Govinda replied from the other side of the tree trunk in a broken voice. It was clear that he had been crying.

"Govinda. What's wrong?" BJ asked with genuine concern in his voice. He did the opposite of what the young Swiss man asked him to do and sat down cross-legged next to him.

Govinda had evidently been holding back the tears. Upon feeling

BJ's empathy, he began bawling without restraints. BJ didn't know how to respond. He'd experienced more emotion in the four weeks of training at the ashram than ever before. All he could do was sit still and let Govinda cry.

When he began to calm down, Govinda became self-conscious. He wiped the tears from his face and sat up, trying to look dignified.

"I am sorry," Govinda said. "I shouldn't have lost control like that."

"That's quite alright," BJ said. "You wanna tell me what's going on?"

"Didn't Lulu tell you?"

"Tell me what?"

"That she is leaving?"

"As a matter of fact, she did," BJ replied. "Ohhh," he continued, "you are sad because she is leaving. I knew the two of you were friends, but I wasn't sure if there was anything more to it. Guess there was, based on your reaction."

"Did she tell you what she was going to do?" Govinda stammered, trying to regain control of his breath.

"No, she didn't."

"She is going to Vegas to become a stripper," Govinda said with pain and anger in his voice. "A stripper! Can you believe that?"

BJ was astonished.

"Her goal is to work in Vegas for a few years," Govinda continued, "and earn enough money to go back to school so that she can become a nurse. She just got back from auditioning there. Said she made between five hundred and one thousand dollars per night. Told me she'll be set for a long time..."

Govinda's voice broke again, but he stifled the urge to cry.

"That's an interesting choice," was all that BJ could think to say.

"Interesting? Interesting!" Govinda cried. "She is leaving me, us, for that. She's becoming a sex worker, there is no denying that. Sure, we were not exactly a couple. Gurudev told me to court her and not have sex with her, but she showed signs, talked about how great it would be if we could live like Yogi Krishna and Lilavati."

"Poor guy," BJ responded. "You thought that a woman like that would want to live like Lilavati?"

"That's what she said," Govinda replied, teeth clenched.

"Sorry to break it to you pal, but women lie," BJ stated in the most empathetic tone he could muster.

"Arrgghhhh," Govinda cried, "I am so angry, so sad, so frustrated, I could —"

"Don't do anything rash," BJ interrupted. "She broke a promise. It happens. You still have your practice, your guru, and your goal in life, to uncover that which does not change. Just breathe through this. A few weeks from now, you'll be okay."

"It doesn't feel like it," Govinda replied, looking like he had been punched in the gut.

"Believe me, I understand. Heartbreak is painful. Not more than a year ago I left my long-term girlfriend, the mother of my children, for another woman, but even if I chose to leave, it was still difficult. Anytime you need to talk, feel free to tap me on the shoulder. I know I am only here for six more days, but —"

Govinda looked up, still teary-eyed: "Thanks."

"I am here for you," BJ replied, then added, "my friend."

The two men sat side by side under the olive tree. For the first time since his arrival, BJ was not bothered by the incessant insect noises that surrounded them, rather he maintained his composure while Govinda gradually regained control of his breathing.

"We'll be late for class," Govinda finally said.

"That's okay," BJ replied. "The main thing is that you need to calm down before you go back. You need to make sure that you don't verbally attack Lulu or become overly agitated when you see her."

Govinda grimaced. "But she promised," he said.

"I know she promised," BJ replied, "but such is the world. People go back on their promises all the time."

"She said —"

"Calm down," BJ commanded. "Breathe in. Breathe out."

"It's just that, I could see it all so clearly," Govinda continued, looking into the distance, into the future. "We would get married, then Yogi Krishna Soham and Lilavati would retire, and then we would run the ashram together, me and her."

"Yeah," BJ replied, "it sucks, it really does, but she has to live her life, and you have to live yours." He paused. "We will stay here together until you are ready to go back."

"It's so unfair."

"I know," BJ said and patted Govinda on the back. "I know."

Chapter Twenty-Six

"I see you are feeling better, Edna," BJ said as he sat down cross-legged on the middle of the floor in the yoga hall, getting ready for an evening lecture with Yogi Krishna Soham.

The middle of the floor!

He hadn't been sitting up against the wall for a whole week now and couldn't hide the pride he was feeling.

"The itching subsided yesterday," Edna replied, smiling with relief. "I just wish my cheating husband would have felt a little bit of the physical torture I went through because of these bites, not to mention the emotional toll his behavior has taken."

"I understand," BJ replied sheepishly. Suddenly, he felt shame, becoming acutely aware of the pain he caused Hafdís, the mother of his children, when he started seeing Sara the previous year.

"There is something oddly poetic about this, though," Edna mused. "My anger at him ends up hurting myself. As much as I would want him to feel my pain, the more I think about it, the more pain it causes me. The Buddha was right when he said that being angry at another person is like picking up hot coals to throw at them, you are the only one that ends up getting burned."

"Funny," BJ replied. "I read that same quote in a book on the coffee table yesterday."

"Too true, isn't it?"

The two of them sat in silence as the room slowly populated.

"Can you believe it?" Laurie said, planting herself in between Edna and BJ, dropping her notebook on the floor. "It's Thursday already. Only three days left. Part of me feels like this has been an endless stay, another part of me feels like I just got here yesterday."

"Funny how time works like that," Edna replied.

"Three days," BJ repeated.

"Yeah," Laurie replied in a spirited voice. "I already have two interviews lined up for yoga teaching when I get back to Texas. I sent a couple of pictures to several studios. One was of me doing the scorpion pose and the other of me posing on one leg in the dancer. Evidently, they liked what they saw. I am soo excited."

"Good for you," Edna replied. "I don't know if I'll ever work as a yoga teacher, but considering my current circumstances, I might just do it on the side."

"Have you decided?" Laurie quizzed. "Are you divorcing Paul?"

"No, I haven't decided," Edna responded. "I am a lawyer after all, so I don't want to make decisions like that during a period of emotional turmoil. No, the two of us need to talk, and I need a clear, calm head to be able to make choices about my future."

"I would have kicked him out already," Laurie said defiantly.

"Of course, you would have," Edna replied in a dismissive tone.

"No, really."

"You say that now, but no one knows what they will do until they are in the situation, faced with the choices."

Andrea sat down next to BJ, away from Edna and Laurie, and whispered: "What are you guys talking about?"

"The future," he whispered back.

"Edna hasn't decided yet?"

"Nope."

Govinda entered the room, as sullen as ever, and sat down next to the stage. By now, that was enough of a cue. The group quieted down.

Shortly after that, Yogi Krishna Soham walked in and sat on stage. He closed his eyes and the students followed suit. For approximately five minutes there was absolute silence, except for the chirping crickets and far away rolling thunder.

The room was unusually muggy. It seemed as if Yogi Krishna and Lilavati were purposefully raising the temperature to save energy as the program wore on.

Yogi Krishna Soham chanted Aum three times, and the group joined in. Then he placed his hands in prayer pose and said: Namaste!

The group responded in kind. He looked across the room, his eyes as kind as they'd been on the day that the group arrived.

"Three days," he said in a low voice. "That is all the time we have left together, this time around."

Everyone nodded.

"Tonight," he continued, raising his voice slightly, "I want to speak to you about several of the dangers you will face on the spiritual path. Of course, I could simply say that everything that changes is an obstacle on the path, but that version would be too general. There are some things which change that produce more obstacles than others."

Yogi Krishna took a sip of his water and wiped his brow.

"Remember when I spoke about Arjuna, the warrior, in my talk about the *Bhagavad-Gita*?"

His question was met with nods and yesses.

"In spiritual terms, his battle was not external. In spiritual terms, his battle was internal. Killing his kinsmen was a metaphor for killing his own attachments. He was waging an internal war with his own demons, his fears, animal instincts and longings, his hatred."

Yogi Krishna looked deeply into the eyes of each of the students. The only one who didn't meet his gaze was Govinda, who seemed almost catatonic, staring at the floor like he was staring into an endless abyss.

"All of you are Arjuna," the yoga master finally declared. "All of you are waging internal wars. I have seen it. Especially during the latter half of our time together."

The students seemed taken aback.

"Don't you believe me?" he continued. "I could take examples, but there is no need to embarrass anyone. Each person here is fighting an internal war of one sort or another, yes?"

Reluctantly, everyone in the room agreed.

"That is the spiritual path," Yogi Krishna declared. "A continual internal war that can only be won by using spiritual tactics and methods. We are our own fiercest enemy, and yet, we must fight peacefully, so as not to destroy ourselves in the process."

He let his words sink in.

"And, as with any war, we can only win if we know the enemy, if we can prepare for potential dangers, and if we can be aware of upcoming perils and pitfalls. That is why, tonight, I want to name a few universal stumbling blocks that you will inevitably encounter if you choose to pursue this path towards enlightenment. Take out your notebooks. It's time to write."

It took a moment for the group to respond, but within two minutes everyone had opened their notebooks and had a pen in hand.

"First obstacle, escapism," Yogi Krishna said while stroking his beard. "Many people use spiritual life as a guise to escape the world. They stop paying their bills, stop taking care of their children, and stop taking their work seriously. In essence, they stop participating in society. Their spiritual practice becomes like yet another drug."

Kurt raised his hand.

"Yes, mister Kurt."

"Isn't that what retreating to a monastery or becoming one of the cave- and forest dwellers you keep referring to is all about? Isn't that the stated goal of spiritual practice, to retreat from the ever-changing world?"

"That is a good observation, mister Kurt, and the answer to your questions is both yes and no. I am not referring to monks and forest dwellers tonight. I am talking about the people who choose to live in the world, who choose to have a job and start a family. For them, escapism is an obstacle. They cannot have it both ways. Either their spiritual path is renunciation, or their path is service. If they renounce, they leave the world behind. If they stay in the world, they serve. However, trying to have it both ways is a recipe for failure. A person who uses escapism is always trying to flee the battle and becomes a deserter to his own cause."

"Okay," Kurt replied, "I think I understand that. It's like committing to therapy halfway and then retreating anytime one comes into contact with uncomfortable emotions, right?"

"Exactly," Yogi Krishna replied, then allowed the students to finish writing before he continued.

"Another obstacle is vanity," he continued. "Vanity can take many shapes, from the most common, typically physical vanity — falling in love with oneself in the mirror, something that happens too often when one focuses only on yoga postures — to the less common, such as taking great pride in one's humility."

"If I may Yogi," Edna offered during Yogi Krishna's pause, "there is a story in Catholicism about a parish priest who was kneeling in front of the altar, proclaiming to God that he was not worthy, that he was nothing. Upon seeing this, his assistant immediately kneeled beside him and began participating in the proclamation. I am not worthy, I am not worthy, the two men said. Then a cleaning lady entered the church. Upon seeing the two priests prostrating before the altar, she also rushed to their side and began declaring that she was not worthy. The assistant then leaned towards the priest and whispered: Look who thinks she's not worthy now."

Edna's delivery caused the students to laugh. Yogi Krishna joined in.

"Very good, miss Edna," he said catching his breath, "very good. I will have to use that story sometime. It demonstrates my point exactly, that one can also become vain and take pride in one's ability to be humble. Note, that a person without vanity cannot be insulted or humiliated. During serious spiritual training in India, the guru rains insults upon the students to remove vain attachments, to remind the student that all those things that can be insulted are not that which does not change. In the West, this method is considered bullying, which is why I do not engage in it any longer, but it is a valuable practice nonetheless."

"Like tough love given to an alcoholic or addict," Thomas chimed in.

"From what I have heard, yes," Yogi Krishna responded.

"But isn't it better to be a little vain and take care of one's health than to dismiss it altogether?" Valentina asked with concern in her voice. "I mean, I could easily see the lack of vanity turn into apathy. From my own experience, a little bit of vanity is a necessary ingredient if I am to will myself to exercise and refuse certain foods."

"She raises an interesting point," BJ concurred. "Isn't a little bit of vanity better than complete apathy?"

"If those were the only two choices, yes, then a little bit of vanity would be better," Yogi Krishna concurred, "but those are not the only two choices. Residing in the bliss of that which does not change is central for the spiritual aspirant. Only when that is not a fundamental practice does this kind of confusion arise. If consciousness is body-centric, then the choice is between vanity and apathy. If, however, consciousness is spirit-centric, then there is no confusion because both vanity and apathy are obstacles that need to be removed."

"But if you remove everything," Andrea said with irritation in her voice, "then there is nothing left."

"Precisely!" Yogi Krishna exclaimed. "When you remove everything there is nothing left, except that which does not change. That is the point of spiritual practice."

"I give up," Andrea responded. "You've been saying that from day one and I still don't get it. I live in a world that changes. That's the way it is. Isn't it better to accept that than to chase this philosophy of something that does not change?"

Yogi Krishna looked her deeply in the eyes and said: "The core of who you are does not change. Having a first-hand experience of that is called enlightenment. Trying to understand it mentally will never work. That is why practice is more important than philosophy. At the same time, we need philosophy to point the way, to remind us of the spiritual goal in this ever-changing world. Yes, the changing world is where you spend your time, but once you are enlightened, you live from the perspective of that which does not change. You know that you are an unchanging being in an ever-changing world."

Andrea shook her head in resistance: "I still don't get it."

"That's okay," Yogi Krishna said with empathy. "I have devoted my entire life to this practice, and sometimes I don't get it either, but, thankfully, I have had enough encounters with that part of me, the part that does not change, to know the truth, to stay the course even when I am confused."

"What are some of the other obstacles?" Thomas queried, wanting to stay on track.

"Laziness is an obstacle," Yogi Krishna replied, "because it keeps the spiritual aspirant from practicing, and only through practice can he or she have the kind of firsthand experience I just referred to. Another obstacle is a lack of patience and persistence. The spiritual aspirant must persist. Ethical deterioration is also an obstacle, when the aspirant begins to discount his or her own behavior, judging ethical standards as not important."

"It sounds like you are describing tamas and rajas qualities as obstacles," Poppy said to everyone's surprise. She rarely took part in philosophical discussions, going so far one time as to brand herself as not a thinker but a doer.

"How observant of you, miss Poppy," Yogi Krishna replied, as astonished as everyone else. "Yes, the obstacles are either degrading and lethargic, tamasik, or egocentric and erratic, rajasik. Again, in simplest terms, obstacles on the spiritual path draw attention away from that which does not change."

"So," BJ quipped, "even this lecture, this program, could be considered as an obstacle."

"You joke, mister BJ, but the answer is yes. If the program does not set you on a path to uncover that which does not change, it will conversely provide you with mental, emotional and physical attachments that could very well veil your eternal spirit even more. Yoga is about the direction of consciousness, not mere actions or thoughts. Even yoga postures and yoga philosophy, applied with the wrong direction of consciousness, can create deep attachments to the ever-changing world, and if that happens, the spirit of yoga is lost, the purpose is defeated."

"When I listen to you, Yogi Krishna," BJ replied, "it seems that very few people in the world practice yoga from the perspective that you teach. It appears that the spirit of yoga is already lost."

"Only one out of a thousand searches for the truth, says Krishna in the Gita. One out of a thousand. If you are that one, then it is your duty to be there for the next person who is one out of a thousand. A real yoga teacher does not concern himself too much with the thousand, but rather with the one."

"That doesn't sound like a very good way to make a living as a yoga teacher," Laurie blurted out.

"It is a delicate balancing act, miss Laurie," Yogi Krishna replied with a smile, "appealing to the masses while staying true to the spirit of yoga, but I have trust in you." He looked at the group. "I have trust in all of you."

Chapter Twenty-Seven

"I can't wait to get home," BJ said to Sara, holding the payphone receiver to one ear, sweating profusely in the ninety-five degree, eighty-five percent humidity steam bath that was enveloping the Florida peninsula that day. "I'll be leaving here on Sunday afternoon and should be in Iceland early Monday morning."

"I'll be there to pick you up."

"You better be. Living like a monk hasn't exactly agreed with me."

"So, you're no longer entertaining the whole celibacy idea?"

"I never was, not seriously anyway."

"I am glad to hear it. Going without sex for more than five weeks doesn't exactly agree with me either."

There was a brief pause when both of them let their imaginations run wild.

"Bjarni?"

"Yes."

"Have you spoken to your dad this week?"

"Yes, on Monday. Why do you ask?"

"I saw him yesterday. He doesn't look well at all."

"He says he's getting better. Says he want's to return to sea on Monday. My mom says he's doing fine."

"Well, I just thought I'd let you know. Have you heard from the kids?"

"Yeah. They'll be staying with us from Thursday to Monday after I get home. You okay with that?"

"Do I have a choice?"

"Not really. We can still get a sitter on Friday or Saturday and go out."

"I'd like that."

About twenty minutes into the phone call, there was a long

pause, a natural occurrence in most of their conversations, a time when they had spoken about day-to-day activities and had to search for new things to talk about.

"Any other news?" BJ finally asked.

"Nothing but gossip," Sara replied, "stuff that I know you're not interested in."

"Well, give it a try. Andrea has been encouraging me to be more curious."

"Okay, so you know my friend Þórhildur, who got divorced last year?"

"Yeah."

"She's been partying ever since, always dragging our friends out with her. Now two of her girlfriends are getting divorced as well. They say they want to have as much fun as she's having, say they want a break from the kids every other weekend."

"That's just sad."

"You wanna hear the clincher?"

"Sure."

"Þórhildur told me the other day that she made a mistake. She says she wants to get married again, doesn't like being on the market."

"So, you're saying that she ruined her own marriage, and torpedoed the marriage of two of her friends, but now she thinks she made a mistake."

"Yep, pretty crazy, huh?"

"Yeah, pretty crazy. Now I remember why I don't like gossip."

BJ walked slowly back to the ashram and got back in time for the two o'clock Friday lecture.

After the lecture, Thomas taught a masculine afternoon yoga class, using plenty of upper body strength throughout, prompting grumbles from several of the women. His posture routine was followed with a long relaxation, during which BJ wasn't sure whether or not he fell asleep, but he came out of it feeling rejuvenated.

To his delight, Lilavati had made BJ's favorite ashram dinner, broccoli, and potatoes in curry, lentil soup, and naan bread.

After dinner, he sat in the dining hall with Kurt and Thomas, waiting for the night's Satsang and lecture.

"I'm gonna miss you guys," he said. "Our conversations have provided me with more intellectual stimulation than I have experienced at any previous point in my life."

"Agreed," Kurt replied. "It's rare indeed to find such good company."

"Can we stay in touch, maybe use Skype?" Thomas asked earnestly. "I don't have many friends that I can talk to like this in Colorado, only my teacher, and that relationship isn't exactly on equal footing. He'll always be more my teacher than a friend."

"We can try," BJ responded, "but we'll need to be organized about it, meet at the same time every week or every other week. If it starts to falter, then we'll cancel. The few other times I have tried this kind of long distance friendship it faded within a year."

"I am willing to commit," Kurt stated.

"So am I," Thomas concurred.

"Good," BJ replied. "Then I'm in. Already looking forward to it."

As the three men sat on the dining room floor, sipping their tea in silence, Govinda burst into the room.

"BJ!" he cried, sounding out of breath. "I've been looking all over for you. Come quickly. There is a phone call for you from Iceland."

BJ jumped up off the floor and ran after Govinda, who headed straight for the home of Yogi Krishna Soham and Lilavati, both of whom stood at the door, waiting. BJ could tell by the looks on their faces that he should expect bad news. They didn't say a word, merely pointed to the telephone on the small table in the foyer. With a sense of foreboding, BJ grabbed the receiver.

"Hello."

"Bjarni, thank God they found you."

"Mom. What's wrong? Is dad back in the hospital?"

"Bjarni," his mother replied, her voice as calm as he'd ever heard it. "Your father has passed away."

"What!"

"This evening. He went out for a walk. They found him lying on the pier next to his ship. It was a heart attack."

BJ had played this moment in his head many times after his father had gone to the hospital the first time. He'd imagined himself breaking down, crying, shouting at the heavens, but now, confronted with his death, BJ felt numb, and, to his surprise, his mother was as composed and collected as he'd ever heard her.

"I'll be on the first flight out tomorrow," was the only thing he could think of saying.

"No need, Bjarni. It's only one day. Finish your training. He's not going anywhere. I already have people helping me with the funeral preparations."

"But I should be with you."

"You will be soon enough."

Silence.

"Bjarni?"

"Yes, mom."

"We'll be okay. Your father was a good man, and we'll miss him, but we'll be okay."

"Yes, mom."

After a few additional word exchanges with his mother, BJ stood motionless in the foyer, suddenly overwhelmed by the smell of sage and turmeric. Govinda had left, but Yogi Krishna and Lilavati still stood next to him.

"Why don't come over here and sit down," Lilavati finally said.

She ushered him into a small room filled with pillows and paintings of a goddess—later identified as Parvati, the goddess of love and devotion. BJ and Yogi Krishna sat down while Lilavati lit candles.

"How did he die, your father?" Yogi Krishna asked respectfully.

"Heart attack, on the pier next to his ship."

"That is a good way to die."

"How do you mean?"

"You have told us that he was a captain of a ship. He died painlessly close to something that he loved dearly. That is a good way to die."

"I guess. I've never thought about death in those terms."

Lilavati sat down next to her husband.

"Tell us about him," she urged gently, "your father."

"He was…"

He was. Those were daunting words.

"Go on," Yogi Krishna said. Calming vibrations emanated from the older couple as they gave him their undivided attention.

"He was… a strong man. Old school. Never showed much emotion, but he loved us, me and my mom. He was away from home a lot, but when he was home, he taught me how to fish, how to fix my car, how to paint, how to hunt."

BJ took a deep breath.

"He told great stories — I mean, great stories. Some of his friends told me over the years that they would much rather have lived my father's version of events than gone through what actually happened. He knew how to dramatize, exaggerate, impress…"

A wave of emotion swept over BJ, and he started crying. Yogi Krishna and Lilavati did nothing. They didn't try to comfort him, didn't try to hug him, didn't try to explain anything away, but rather, they held a space for him and allowed him to experience his emotions. For hours this went on. BJ told stories, then wept, told stories, then wept, all to the undivided attention of the old couple. They were completely there for him, without drama.

Finally, when it was almost midnight, BJ found his way back to his sleeping quarters. Lying in bed, he didn't feel the need to weep or think. His body was completely calm as he stared at the wood panel supporting the mattress in the bunk above him. Every now and then he closed his eyes, but sleep did not come. Strangely enough, he felt completely refreshed when Govinda rang the bell at five-thirty the following morning.

Chapter Twenty-Eight

Predictably, the group rallied around BJ on Saturday after hearing the news of his father's passing. Kurt and Thomas sat with him every chance they got throughout the day. Andrea gave him repeated hugs, then shook her head and covered her face with her hands. To the untrained eye, she appeared more upset than he was. Valentina stopped her freeze out of him, even offered another healing session, which he accepted during the break between breakfast and the written test. Laurie dropped her teasing routine and became genuinely empathetic. Poppy could not hold back the tears, feeling deeply for him because of her mother's passing earlier in the year. Edna spoke empathetically and pointed out several legal issues that he would need to be aware of when he got back. Everyone pulled from his or her own strengths to support BJ during his time of need. Even Govinda came out of his shell, put aside his pouting over Lulu's departure, and gave BJ his sympathies. Yogi Krishna offered him to skip the written test, but BJ pressed on, said it would keep his mind busy.

During lunch hour, BJ was allowed to make calls from Yogi Krishna's home. He talked to Sara and his mother for the entire break. He was surprised when he realized that Lilavati was nowhere to be found. Govinda said that she had left earlier that morning, and he did not know when she would return. Valentina and Thomas were put in charge of making dinner. They made tomato based pasta with tofu and garlic bread. After dinner, the group gathered for their final Satsang together.

"Although these are trying times," Yogi Krishna said, sitting in an unusual pose, up against the wall, with his legs sprawled out before him, "we shall continue as planned."

He seemed unlike himself, distant somehow.

"During this, our last Satsang together, it is customary to give you, the student-teachers, an opportunity to share some of what you have learned during your stay here at the ashram. We are not in a hurry, so take your time. When you are not speaking, give your complete attention to the person who is. Who knows, maybe their discovery about the program or about themselves can be of value to you. Who wants to begin?"

"I'll do it," Poppy said, wearing her now traditional white garbs, with her hair tied back in a ponytail, her black and graying root showing. "I was the first one to speak up when the program began five weeks ago. I might as well be the first to speak now."

"Go ahead, miss Poppy."

"As you know, I came here to supplement my career as an aerobics teacher, to learn new physical techniques to teach my students and perhaps to use those same techniques on my own aging body. Physically, I've gotten everything from this program I expected to get, and for that I am grateful—but my greatest lesson came when I shed the mask that I have worn from the time I remember. I am no longer the one-dimensional Peppy Poppy I have always been. I am allowing myself to feel, to be, to see, to think… all things I did not do before I came here. During our time together, I have become a fuller person. I want to thank all of you for not judging me, for allowing me to go through my transformation."

The group responded with bows of respect, telling her that she was welcome.

"And I want to thank you specifically, Yogi Krishna Soham, for opening up a new world to me. I want to ask you to be my guru—if you will have me—so that I can continue to receive guidance on this spiritual path which I have embarked upon."

"I am already your guru, miss Poppy," Yogi Krishna said sitting up slightly, "and will continue to be there for you if you need me."

Poppy smiled.

"Thank you," she said. "I'm done."

"Who's next?" Yogi Krishna asked, his tone revealing a hint of sadness.

"I'll go," Andrea said. "This program has done wonders for my body. I feel better in my own skin than I have ever felt. All of you may not see it, but I have lost weight and feel much stronger. On the other hand, I am not sure about all this 'that which does not change' stuff. Maybe I'll understand it when I come home. I do look forward to teaching yoga poses, breathing techniques and relaxation to my students. All of you have been great. I hope that we can stay in touch. That's all I have to say. Andrea, out," she said, put two fingers over her lips and simulated dropping the microphone with her other hand.

"You joker, you," Laurie responded laughing. "I'm gonna miss you. I'm gonna miss all you guys, especially Thomas's strong hands, which have saved my back and shoulders from becoming too stiff after all this sitting."

Laurie glanced at Thomas, who looked away.

"Alright, miss Laurie," Yogi Krishna said. "Since you are already speaking, you might as well be next. What have you learned?"

"What have I learned," the young woman replied tongue in cheek. "I've learned that there can be a lot of drama when a group of adults is forced to live together without electronics for five weeks."

She laughed.

"No, no, I'm kidding," she added, "but not really. Y'all are some messed up people. I like that about you."

"Miss Laurie, please stick to telling us what you have learned," Yogi Krishna pressed her rather impatiently.

"Okay. I'm sorry," Laurie replied with a bow. "So, I have learned a great deal about yoga poses, for which I am grateful, about cleansing, from which I am hoping to recover, and about that which does not change, although I must confess, that like Andrea, I am not sure I understand that completely. Most importantly — and I am completely serious now — I have learned that I, at twenty-four, can be without my electronics for five weeks. I did not think I could do that. That was good. All in all, I feel that this has been a good program. Thank you."

"Thank you, miss Laurie. Who's next?"

"I'll go," Thomas said and scratched his goatee for a moment before he continued. "Although I was a yoga teacher when I came here, this program has added several new dimensions to my understanding and practice of yoga. I was glad to realize that in most cases, you and my other teacher, Yogi Vasudev, were in complete harmony with each other and that the differences were minuscule. I look forward to melding what I have learned into my own style of teaching and will borrow heavily from your training when I design my own yoga teacher program, although it will not be residency training like yours, more like an apprenticeship, where the students teach alongside me at my studio. Your teachings have been invaluable, Yogi Krishna Soham. Thank you."

"You are most welcome, mister Thomas. Please keep me updated on your progress and feel free to contact me if you have any questions or think I can help with your training."

"Thank you," Thomas said, put his hand in prayer pose and bowed. "Namaste!"

"I'll go next," Valentina offered.

Yogi Krishna nodded his approval.

"We haven't always seen eye to eye, you and I," Valentina said, forcing a smile, "but I have to admit that you are a genuine teacher. You are true to your word and consistent in your teachings. I respect that."

Yogi Krishna placed his hands in prayer pose and bowed slightly, like he were saying, thank you.

"This program has taught me plenty about yoga philosophy and yoga postures," she continued, "but during the last few weeks I have learned something about myself, which I was previously unaware of, and this discovery, in and of itself, was worth the entire time I spent here."

Valentina took a deep breath and steadied herself.

"This confession of mine may sound conceited, but in my interactions with BJ here, I realized that I have, for far too long, seen my beauty as a burden. Yes, I know I am beautiful. I've been told that all my life. Told that I was lucky, that I was exceptional. More men than I can count have courted me. By all accounts, beauty provides an advantage in our society. However, when I first gave BJ a healing session, which was after his father was admitted into the hospital three weeks ago, I sincerely wanted to be his friend. But, when I felt his amorous intentions towards me, it set off a domino effect, reminding me of all the times during which my beauty had impeded me from having normal friendly relationships with men. Not once in my life have I had a male friend. Not once. I shut BJ out as a result — I'm sorry about that BJ — but every time I saw him and Andrea being chummy, I was reminded that I could never have that. And so, that has been my internal struggle, my internal war, during these past few weeks. I am slowly coming to terms with it, but the realization hurt deeply."

The group took a moment to internalize the confession.

"I've never had any male friends either," Laurie finally blurted out, "but I can get men to do pretty much whatever I want them to do. That's a plus."

"It's fun for a while, Laurie," Valentina responded, "but now, at my age, I long for deeper cerebral relationships. Women generally see me as a threat and men see me as a sex object, so I never get honest relations with either sex. Look, I know that complaining about my beauty sounds vain, maybe even inconsiderate, seeing as many of you have heavier crosses to bear, but this was my big discovery during this training, and I decided to share it, to come clean."

"I've only ever been friends with men, Valentina," Andrea said, "all my life and none of them have ever seen me as a sex object. That's pretty hurtful as well, but I appreciate hearing your point of view. I've never thought about beauty like that before."

"I—" BJ started to say.

"You don't have to say anything BJ," Valentina responded before he could get further. "It's not your fault. In fact, I should thank you for being the one who caused this chain reaction. Who knows where this self-discovery will lead."

"Know thyself," Yogi Krishna added, "that is our motto here. Thank you for confiding in us, miss Valentina. Every new piece helps complete the puzzle."

"Namaste, Yogi Krishna," Valentina responded. "I'll probably grow to appreciate your teachings even more when I get back to my regular routine and have time to reflect on them."

"Wow! This program has been a psychological goldmine," Kurt began without asking for permission. "I mean, the psychology of yoga, which is disguised as philosophy, has shown me the universality of man's afflictions. To think that these ideas were passed down over a period of thousands of years. I must say that connecting the three major paths of yoga to psychological drivers that are still in place — needs for action, emotion, and intellect — was and remains brilliant. Furthermore, the chakras have helped me put certain psychological complications into perspective and shown me new areas to work on, both for my patients and myself. I plan to incorporate all of that, plus the breathing, relaxation and meditation techniques you have taught us, Yogi Krishna."

Kurt kept fidgeting with his glasses as he spoke, pushing them higher onto his nose, running his fingers up and down the sides of the rims.

"And this group," he continued. "I have learned a ton, both from my conversations with my roommates and from the interactions I have observed during our stay here. I can't thank all of you enough for your honesty and ability to communicate at a high level. This mix of people — especially the seven of you, who have been here for the entire time — has created unique circumstances for learning and discovery."

"Thanks, Kurt," Andrea replied on behalf of the group. "I'm not sure if what you said about us is good or bad, seeing as we've all been dealing with some problems while here, but thanks. We appreciate you as well."

"Oh," Kurt replied, "I most definitely mean it in a good way. I have been inspired by your ability to bare your souls while surrounded by strangers. It takes me months to get to this level of open communications with my patients."

"Namaste, Kurt." Yogi Krishna said.

"Namaste, Yogi."

"Edna," Yogi Krishna said, switching his attention, "would you like to go next and tell us what you have learned during your stay here?"

"Sure," she replied. "I have been thinking about that a lot while listening to all of you, about what I learned here in addition to yoga postures and yoga philosophy. I've come up with two things that I think are important. First, I learned that I am enough, that I don't need anything or anybody to be who I am. That is huge for me. I used to need praise and love like others need oxygen. In the past, I never spent much time alone, and when I did, I usually had the TV or radio on so that I wouldn't need to be alone with my thoughts. Here, I have spent large chunks of time alone, and I have learned to like my own company. I am enough. I can be alone."

Andrea, Laurie, and Valentina responded with nods and empathetic yesses.

"Thanks, ladies," Edna replied, "as nice as that is to hear, it is also good to know that I don't need that kind of encouragement anymore. I will accept it when given, but I will no longer search for it. The second thing I learned was how to breathe through pain. When I found out that Paul had cheated on me, it was a shock. I could hardly breathe and went out for a run to clear my head. You know how that turned out. The ant bites were excruciatingly painful, all fifty-seven of them. They burned and stung and itched something awful. The physical pain combined with the emotional upheaval seemed more than I could bear, but somehow I survived. That taught me a valuable lesson as well," she said and smiled. "I can breathe through pain."

"There are limits," Yogi Krishna said. "I tried to breathe through a root canal once," he added with a witty smile, "it didn't work."

Nerves were raw, and the room exploded with laughter—even

BJ found himself smiling.

"I'll make sure to know my limits," Edna replied when she caught her breath. "Thank you, Yogiji. I appreciate all that you have done for me — for us."

When everyone in the room had settled down, all eyes were on BJ.

"Would you like to share BJ?" Yogi Krishna asked tentatively. "You don't have to, but seeing as you have insisted on participating in everything today, I have to ask."

BJ looked up.

"Yeah, sure, I'd like to share," he said in a hoarse voice, sounding like he'd been at an exciting sporting match the night before. "I want to thank you all for being there for me today. I guess the full weight of my dad's passing will not hit me until I get back home, but... "

He took a deep breath.

"I am a skeptic, Yogi Krishna," he continued, "so even though your presentation of Atman, as that which does not change, has been rational and logical from day one, I have had a hard time believing in the concept. Sure, I thought to myself, we might be able to find peace of mind every now and then, but a non-changing part of ourselves, I doubted that very much, until last night."

Yogi Krishna leaned forward and listened intently.

"Last night, when you and Lilavati sat with me, allowed me to cry and talk and sit in silence, there was a presence there that I can't explain. You held a comforting space for me, something I have never experienced before. It was neither emotional nor apathetic. It felt like pure awareness, witnessing, allowing. I don't have the words to explain it."

Yogi Krishna nodded knowingly.

"It was that which does not change, wasn't it?"

"That which does not change is always present," Yogi Krishna replied. "Your emotional state last night just allowed you to experience it."

Chapter Twenty-Nine

Graduation day. Sunday morning. The group had slept in until seven o'clock and then headed straight for breakfast. Lilavati was nowhere to be seen, so they rustled up some toast, cereal, and granola. After breakfast, it was time to pack. The graduation ceremony would begin at ten o'clock, and soon thereafter airport shuttles and cars would start arriving to pick up the graduates.

Thomas, Kurt, and BJ were quick to pack their things and clean their room. When they were done, they helped Govinda with other chores around the ashram. It was their final seva.

Just before ten, the group was gathered in the yoga hall, all dressed in white, along with Rukmini, Tiffany, and Jaipur Mehta, all of whom had frequented the ashram during the advanced portion of the teacher training. The room was sparsely decorated with a few candles and only two vases filled with fresh flowers. Lilavati's presence was missed in more ways than one.

At ten minutes past ten, the group was getting restless. Neither Govinda nor Yogi Krishna were in attendance yet.

"Does anyone know where they are?" Laurie called over the room.

Her question was met with shaking heads.

Finally, at fifteen minutes past the hour, Govinda arrived with a stack of graduation certificates in hand. He sat down next to the stage and muttered that Yogi Krishna would be coming shortly. Rukmini decided to take matters into her own hands and began chanting the mantra that they knew so well, Om Namo Bhagavate Vasudevaya. Soon, the group followed her lead, swaying, clapping their hands, and singing in harmony.

When Yogi Krishna Soham finally entered the room ten minutes later, wearing his traditional hemp clothes rather than his ceremonial white attire, the singing stopped abruptly. In fact, the room became so quiet that loud creaking noises could be heard while he arranged his legs in the lotus pose. He looked up with sadness in his eyes.

"Today, you graduate," he said, in an uncharacteristically shaky voice. "It should be a joyous occasion. You have all done well. You should be proud. I know that I am proud of each and every one of you."

He cleared his throat, took a deep breath and continued.

"I hope you will remember all the good that has happened at the ashram, all the good things that you have learned here, even after I tell you…"

The students looked around at each other in confusion.

"Just remember," he continued after clearing his throat once again, "that my personal weaknesses should not, no, they do not in any way reflect on you or your yoga degree."

"No matter what has happened, Gurudev," Rukmini stated in her ceremonial tone, "I will never leave your side."

"Thank you, Rukmini. You are a trusted disciple."

He lifted his gaze from Rukmini and looked across the room, into the eyes of each of the graduates, just like he had done on day one, except that this time the gaze was not filled with loving kindness, rather with a profound sense of sorrow.

"Lilavati is not here," he finally said. "Yesterday morning I told her something which I am not proud of, something I should have told her months ago. She decided that she needed some space. She decided that she needed to—"

Yogi Krishna's words were interrupted by a loud knock on the door.

"Govinda, would you get that please?" Yogi Krishna asked.

The young man stood up quickly and ran to the front door.

"As I was saying," Yogi Krishna Soham continued, but before he could say more, Govinda was back in the room.

"Gurudev! It's the police. They need to speak to you."

Without saying a word, Yogi Krishna arose and walked briskly to the front door.

Rukmini, Andrea, and Laurie stood up to follow him, prompting the entire group of graduates to do the same. Just inside the doorway, there were two detectives already speaking to the yoga master.

"Are you Gopal Dhaduk?"

Yogi Krishna nodded: "Yes, I am. What is this about?"

"We are Detectives Smith and Juarez from the Miami PD. We need to ask you a few questions. Would you like to go somewhere private?"

"No. We can talk here," Yogi Krishna replied. "I have nothing to hide from this group."

"Alright then," Detective Smith replied. "Is your wife Lilavati Dhaduk?"

"Yes," Yogi Krishna said. "Is she okay? Did something happen?"

"Do you own a blue Chrysler Town and Country minivan?" Detective Juarez continued without answering Yogi Krishna's question.

"Yes, we do."

"And do you know a miss Alyssa Floros?"

"Sunita," Yogi Krishna replied with concern in his voice. "Yes. I know her. What is this all about?"

"Just a few more questions, sir," Detective Smith said. "Can you tell us the nature of your relationship with miss Floros?"

Yogi Krishna paused for a moment, looking ashamed.

"Yes, she has been a student of mine for several years and is carrying my child. I told my wife about it yesterday."

Carrying his child? He had cheated on Lilavati with Sunita, the little Greek-American? Yogi Krishna's statement was met with audible gasps and headshakes. Rukmini fainted and slid down the wall. Doctorji rushed to her side to help her.

"Are you sure you don't want to go somewhere private, mister Dhaduk?" Detective Juarez asked, pointing to the group that was now in upheaval.

"Yes, I am sure. They are allowed to hear this, whatever it is. They will learn about it sooner or later," Yogi Krishna replied, steadying his voice. "I was about to tell them about my involvement with Sunita before you arrived. Now, can you please tell me what this is about?"

"Yes, sir," Detective Smith replied. "We just needed to check the facts before we proceeded."

"Please, just tell me what happened," Yogi Krishna Soham cried.

"At approximately nine this morning," Detective Juarez proceeded to explain, "we got a call from your wife, Lilavati Dhaduk. She reported that she had willfully hit a pedestrian with her car. We later identified the victim as Alyssa Floros."

"What? She hit Sunita? Is she alright?"

"Miss Floros is recovering," Detective Juarez continued. "She has a broken arm, a minor concussion, and bruises to her hips and legs. She did, however, suffer a miscarriage."

Yogi Krishna looked like he had been punched in the gut. He took a moment to steady himself and then asked: "And my wife?"

"We regret to inform you that your wife, Lilavati Dhaduk," Detective Smith answered, "has been arrested for assault and manslaughter."

Epilogue

"Bjarni! Hey! How are you doing?"

Stretching in a square outside of a trendy Icelandic gym, a concrete structure with ceiling-high tinted windows, getting ready for his midday run, BJ looked up to see who was calling.

"Magnús," he replied gleefully, "I haven't seen you in ages. How have you been, my friend?"

"I've been well," Magnús replied, as he walked up to BJ, dressed in running pants and a fleece jacket with a gym bag slung over his right shoulder. "I was sorry to hear about your father's passing last year."

"Thank you. He died before his time."

"He did. He was a great man."

"Yes, he was."

"Weren't you at some sort of a yoga retreat when he passed away. I remember hearing something about that."

"I was, but I got back three days after his death."

"That's good. I am sorry that I couldn't make it to the funeral. I was on a trip, looking to invest in a fishery in Nigeria."

"Understood."

There was a brief silence while the two estranged childhood friends thought about what to say next.

"I meant to ask you about something when we'd next meet," Magnús said hesitantly. "I hope you don't mind. The yoga guru you studied with, he isn't by any chance —"

"The same guy who has been in the news lately," BJ interrupted. "Yes. I am afraid so."

"I just wanted to confirm. You know how the Internet is these days," Magnús said, chewing on the gossip. "He was cheating, wasn't he, and his wife ran his girlfriend down in their minivan, was convicted of manslaughter or something like that, right?"

"Yes. It was an unfortunate tragedy."

"And you had no idea that it was going on."

"Nope."

Ever since the news broke, becoming a viral sensation — with headlines like 'Guru Cheats and Wife Kills Unborn Child' and 'Cheating Guru Loses Ashram to Pay for Wife's Defense' — BJ had done little else but answer questions about his time in Florida.

"Man, that must have made you angry."

"Not really. At the time when it happened, I was sad because of my father's passing. The whole thing just deepened that feeling of sadness. I never felt betrayed like many of my friends there, maybe because, even if I wanted to, I was never entirely convinced by his celibacy claims."

"Oh," Magnús said, holding back a laugh. "He claimed to celibate as well. Man, this story just keeps getting better."

"There is nothing 'good' about this story Magnús. It's a human tragedy."

"Sorry, Bjarni. You know how it is. I wasn't involved. It just sounds so incredible."

BJ thought about letting his friend squirm a little, but decided against it. Magnús's reaction was not the most offensive he'd encountered — not by a long shot.

"That's okay," BJ sighed. "Unfortunately, these kinds of events aren't as rare as you would think. After I got home, I did some digging, and the number of Eastern gurus — especially men from India and Thailand — who have gotten into trouble because of money, sex, and power is astounding. It seems like these men are tethered to a philosophy that doesn't match reality, a philosophy that is respected in their home countries, where women leave them alone, and they have little access to money, but then they can't withstand the temptations when they come to the West."

"Really? It's that common?"

"It seems so. I found a case of a guru in Texas who fled to Mexico after he was convicted of molesting young women, of a big ashram in Massachusetts that was torn up due to a sex scandal, and of several Zen monks who disrobed because they either slept with their students or misused money."

"Sounds like they suffered from severe cases of premature holiness," Magnús quipped.

"Premature holiness," BJ replied with a strained smile. "Yeah, I guess that's one way of putting it."

He'd begun jogging in place, showing signs that he was getting ready to run.

"Well then," Magnús replied, glad to see that BJ wasn't too offended, looking like he couldn't wait to share his premature holiness joke with his gym buddies, "I won't keep you from your midday run."

"Thanks. It was good to see you. Will you be at our wedding this summer?"

"Of course," Magnús replied. "You and Hafdís. She took you back and agreed to marry you, huh? I wouldn't miss it for the world."

"Yep. Me and Hafdís. The events that happened last year put things into perspective. I realized just how important family is. Plus, we have a lot more in common than Sara and I ever did. I am just lucky that she agreed to take me back, luckier still that she agreed to marry me."

"Not a minute too soon, buddy. You're lucky to have her."

"Don't I know it," BJ replied with a smile and started running. "See you at the wedding."

BJ zipped up his running jacket and embraced the chilly summer breeze as he ran towards a nearby park. He planned to run at least five miles today. It was June, the birch trees were in full bloom, the sun was shining, and the gusts of air felt refreshing.

After three laps around the park, breathing in rhythm his steps, fully immersed in the repetition, a word crept into his awareness — that. Involuntarily, it began repeating in his mind in rhythm with every other step — that, that, that. He kept running. The word consumed his attention — that, that, that. Another lap into the run and he could no longer feel his body like he was running on air. At that moment, he became that which does...

For more about the author visit: *www.authorbergmann.com*

63165219R00112

Made in the USA
Charleston, SC
26 October 2016